JUNKYARD HEART

PORTH EWAN BAY

GARRETT LEIGH

For everyone who was here from the start

AUTHOR NOTE

This book was originally published in 2016, and as such is set in 2016.

For Rebel Kings fans, this is around the time Cam's parents have died, Saint has joined the council full time, and they're navigating what that means for the club.

But it should be noted that Junkyard Heart isn't an RK book. It's Porth Ewan book, which means all the angst and swoon, but none of the violence.

Please heed the trigger warnings for addiction, mental illness, bad break ups, and family drama.

CHAPTER
ONE

Fuck. My. Life.

Tie-dye, chickpeas, and hessian. I scowled at the wigwams and peace signs and wondered how the hell I'd ended up at a bloody hippie love-in at 10 a.m. on a Saturday morning.

You know how.

My gaze fell on the broad shoulders of my favourite brother, and I suppressed a heavy sigh. Gaz had assumed I'd have nothing better to do than lug his junk around Porth Ewan's annual jam festival and, sadly, he'd been right.

Yeah.

Fuck my life.

I picked up the bulging bag, stuffed with jars of artisan preserves, pickles, and condiments, and wove my way through the crowds of crusties. Gaz manned a stall at the back of the food tent, which was in the next field over, and about as far from the festival's entrance as possible.

Not impressed, Gaz. Not impressed.

Like he gave a shit. His mile-wide grin when I finally caught up with him confirmed that he didn't much care that I'd dragged my hungover self out of bed to be his bitch. "Over there, mate." He winked. "Then you can help me here. Davey's gone for breakfast."

"Are you taking the piss?" I dumped the bag at his feet. "I'm not staying. I only brought these because Ma bribed me with a fry-up."

Gaz rolled his eyes. "Such a mammy's boy. At least stick around for a bit, show me some love."

"What do you need my love for?" I pointed at the *Free Hugs* sign attached to the pork pie stall a few metres away. "There's plenty to go round."

"Brat."

Gaz looked like he wanted to call me worse, but a potential customer distracted him, and he was happily diverted, plying them with my stepmother's scones, smothered in his signature rhubarb conserve.

Only Gaz could make WI-style jam and chutney cool. With his funky glasses and scruffy beard, he was the epitome of the wanky hipsters I'd left London to escape.

And the rest.

The image of my ex cosying up to his beautiful wife flashed into my mind. I pushed it away. Fuck that shit. It had been six months. I was over it . . . honest.

"Wake up, you grumpy arse." Gaz nudged me. I'd missed him handing the reins to our middle brother, Davey, and invading my personal space. "What are you up to for the rest of the day?"

"Being *busy*. I've got a job on tonight. Band gig in Porth Luck."

"That's good." Gaz seemed thoughtful, which was always dangerous. "I meant other than work, though. Seriously, bro. You need to get out more. Eat, drink, get laid."

"I got drunk last night, thanks very much."

I left out the part where I'd been home alone.

Gaz ribbed me a little longer before I escaped under the pretence of having a look around, though the smirk he treated me to—and the dead arm that came with it—left me in little doubt that he'd seen through my bullshit.

Not that I cared. This was my time to not give a crap. As a kid, I'd spent most of my school holidays following my dad around these stupid festivals, watching him flog the tiny onions he pickled in the derelict barn on the family farm. But I wasn't a child anymore, and I didn't have the patience for this bollocks.

I wandered out of the food tent and bought a pint from the beer stand. Who cared if it was barely 11 a.m.?

Not me, but despite my best attempt at disinterest, a few things caught my eye as I drifted through the farm hosting the festival: a besom broom maker, and a girl weaving a rug from rags. Behind a bee skep stall, a band warmed up on a small stage. Their collection of weird and wonderful drums intrigued me. But nothing truly held my attention until the deep clatter of motorbike engines shattered the peaceful morning air.

I spun around as six Harleys rumbled into the festival field, easing to a collective stop behind the band tent. I expected the riders to be old men, but as the front bikers pushed their helmets off, I found myself staring at a collection of tattooed men younger than me.

Intrigued, I reached for the camera I'd left at home. Settled for my iPhone, raising it to take a shot—

"I wouldn't." An inked hand attached to a slender tattooed arm lowered my camera for me. "They ain't the kind of people you want to piss off."

I turned my head and fell into a set of greener than green eyes that instantly erased the handsome bikers from my mind.

Dark, windswept hair.

Scruffy jaw.

A slender frame he wore like a dream.

Jesus-fucking-Christ, where had this bloke been all my life?

"Sorry." I found my tongue. "I can't help it when something grabs me."

Like him. But as blindsided as I was by his appearance, I knew better than to point my camera again.

"Come over here." The man's epic bone-structure caught the light of the early morning sun, his deep, Cornish brogue turning my insides to molten fire. "Maybe you'll see something you like."

I'd already seen something I liked, but I let him tow me away from where the bikers had convened and to an eco-furniture stall in a quiet-ish corner of the second field.

Yeah. Okay. He had my attention.

Pausing, I stared at a wardrobe that looked like it had walked out of the Laura Ashley catalogue. What the fuck was so eco-friendly about that? It took me too long to realise it had been crafted from disused warehouse pallets.

Fucking hell.

I circled the wardrobe, studying it from every angle, and tried to find something to feed my inner cynic.

Failed.

The wardrobe was imperfectly perfect, like every other piece of furniture dotted around the sun-faded grass: a bed crafted from stripped tree trunks; a sofa from old tractor tyres; and, my new favourite, a pool table built into the upturned hull of a vintage fishing boat.

The boat was incredible, and I raised my phone again, crouching to get a decent shot of the whole piece as my companion treated me to the low chuckle of my dreams.

"Got a thing for rust?"

I glanced up, squinting in the sunlight again. This dude, his voice was old—*wise*—but his face was around my age and gorgeous enough to erode my power of speech.

"Erm . . ." I scrambled to my feet, lost again in those warm green eyes. "Actually, I do like the rust. The piece would be gimmicky if they'd cleaned the boat up too much."

"Gimmicky, eh?"

"Yeah, like those mirrors you get with seashells around them." I deleted two of my three shots, hyperaware of Hot Bloke still watching. "Or all that fake shabby chic shit you see on the high street."

Hot Bloke laughed. "I don't spend much time on the high street. Here, come and have a look at this."

He gave my arm a tug that sent shock waves through me, but before I could recover, I was transfixed by a rejuvenated slab of an old wooden printing press, framed in dark-brown oak.

"Damn." I took a shot of that too. "It's beautiful."

"You think so? I only finished it last night."

"Finished it? This is your work?"

Hot Bloke shrugged and held out his hand. "Kim Penrose. Pleased to meet you."

"Jas Manning." I shook his hand, absorbing the old Porth Ewan name. *Penrose*. Like the Lusmoores, that clan was built into the land around here. "Nice to meet you too."

"Jas? As in, Jason?"

I rolled my eyes. "It's Jasper, actually, but don't even think about pulling a Brummie accent on me. I've heard all the carrot jokes in the world."

That earned me a grin that made the sun look pale, and Kim laughed too, deep and rumbling. "Not gonna lie, if you'd been a redhead instead of them ebony curls, I might've tried it."

I didn't doubt it for a second. Hot Bloke—*Kim*—had a

mischievous gleam in his eyes that I'd seen many times from my brothers. Not that he reminded me of Gaz or Davey.

Fuck no.

I gave myself an internal shake and gazed around at the rest of the stall's offerings. "So this is your stuff?"

"Aye-aye. Never done this event before, though. We're kinda new."

"To the area?"

"Nah, Porth Ewan born and bred. You?"

I didn't bother to quip that if I'd grown up in Porth Ewan, we'd likely have already crossed paths. Native folk round here didn't take kindly to their tight-knit community being mocked. "I was born here, but I grew up in London with my mum. Only just moved back. My family has been doing these festivals for years, though. There's a lot of them around, if you like that kind of thing."

"We do."

We? I forced myself not to ask the question. Gay, straight, whatever, I'd sworn off men for good.

Forever.

I couldn't help giving Kim a second once-over, though, and I bit back another sigh. Whichever way he swung, he obviously wasn't single. And anyway, I'd finished my pint, so it was time I moved on.

"Anyway..."

Kim caught my arm. "You never said why you were here. Do you have a stall?"

His hand on my skin was electric, stealing my power of speech all over again. "Uh, I'm helping my brother in the food tent."

Those green eyes sparked. Or maybe it was me. "You'll be here all day then?"

I'd had zero intentions to be, but something—everything—about Kim shifted my brain on its axis.

I couldn't contemplate going home.

Instead, I fudged a vague explanation of the family business I'd spent my whole life dodging, and forced myself back to Gaz.

My brother greeted me with barely concealed surprise. "You're still here? Thought you'd sloped off for the day."

"*Moi*?" I slipped behind the bench like I did it all the time. "Just went for a pint. Where do you need me?"

Gaz eyed me with suspicion. "How many pints did you have? Twenty?"

"Piss off."

He relented and passed me an apron. I winced. *Belly Acre Farm*. Side-splitting, eh? My dad had thought so when he'd renamed his Porth Ewan farm in the seventies. And he still thought so now.

The day dragged on. Lunchtime eased into the afternoon, and despite the shackles of jam life heavy around my limbs, it didn't take long to slip into my role. The patter came easy, and time began to tick faster.

It was late by the time Gaz trod on my foot. "You've got company, kiddo."

I looked up from the gooseberry chutney I was relabelling on Gaz's behalf—was it so hard to stick the labels on the right way round?—and found myself face to face with Kim.

His electric grin skewered me. "Got time for a drink?"

"Er . . ." I glanced at Gaz, absorbed his subtle, amused nod, and cleared my throat. "Sure. Let's go."

I escaped the stall and fell into step beside Kim. He didn't say anything at first, and it took me a while to notice he was eying the apron I'd forgotten to ditch.

"Don't start."

He chuckled. "What's your connection to the farm?"

"My dad and his missus own it. And he's to blame for the name. He smoked a lot of weed in the seventies. Still thinks it's hilarious."

Kim smiled. "Nothing wrong with that. My old man wouldn't know fun if it bit him on the arse."

Even with the warmth of the late summer sun, the way his melodic brogue curled around every word made me shiver, and I couldn't help wondering why he'd sought me out. Definitely wasn't my dazzling knowledge of eco-friendly food production, or jaded enthusiasm for Porth Ewan, and I struggled to believe it was my personality.

And the wondering kept me company all the way to the beer tent.

Kim had one of those faces that gave nothing away. He bought me a microbrewery pint and apple juice for himself.

"Not scrumpy?"

He shuddered. "No chance. My mate's dad used to charge us a score for six pints and a pasty. Didn't make it past three for years."

"Did you get the pasty when you got to number six?"

"Something like that. So, you grew up in London?"

"For my sins." I set my pint down and glanced around. The festival had picked up after lunch, and was buzzing now. "My dad hooked up with my mum at a swingers' party. She had me here, then fucked off back to London, taking me with her. I spent most summers on the farm, but I'm a city boy, really."

"Wow." Kim grinned around his glass. "Didn't have that kinky backstory pegged from your jam sales pitch."

"It's the Belly Acre way. Also, as far as jam's concerned, my brothers trained me well. Said I'd end up back here eventually, so I had to learn."

"And they weren't wrong, eh?"

I shook my head, waiting for Kim to ask what had happened to make my brothers' shared prophecy come true, but he didn't. Instead, he looked over my shoulder at the band getting ready for the afternoon performances. "Is that a bassoon?"

"A what?" I followed his gaze to the stage and a mini woodwind section setting up with a folk band I'd seen a hundred times at festivals just like this one. "Wouldn't surprise me with that lot."

Kim shrugged as the air around us vibrated with the rumble of the motorbike horde getting ready to leave. "I like their vibe, but I'm more of a funk-rock bloke to be honest."

That fit with the untamed hair and leather bracelets. "You'd probably like The Mocking Horses then," I said. "They're playing Porth Luck's roundhouse tonight."

"I know. A bunch of us blagged tickets at the last minute."

"Really?" My heart skipped a beat. What were the chances? TMH were one of the hottest bands in the southwest and tickets to their shows were gold dust. I'd been lucky to get a press pass. "I've wanted to shoot them live for ages."

"*Shoot* them?" Kim frowned a second before his face cleared. "Ah . . . and you finally get to tonight, eh?"

"Yup."

Kim stared a long moment before his devilish grin split his face in half, and he nudged me with his knee. "Then I guess I'll see you there."

"Then I guess I'll see you there . . ."

I scouted the concert venue with the words reverberating in my brain. Kim had cut and run soon after he'd uttered them, but they'd stayed with me every minute since, distracting me from just about everything. Not that setting up at the small venue required much brainpower. I'd been shooting bands here since I was sixteen and knew every nook and cranny like the back of my hand.

Still, it had been a while. I hadn't done much live work since I'd moved to Porth Ewan, preferring the solitude of online design contracts—websites, branding, social media—all the corporate bullshit I despised. I'd landed this job by accident after a beer-fuelled meeting down the boozer closest to my folk's farm, and now here I was, observing the sound check as the long-dormant buzz of a grungy band gig seeped into my soul.

That, and the promise of seeing Kim again, but I tried not to think about that.

Tried, with questionable success. It was a coincidence, right? That we were both going to be here? That my spine kept tingling and skin flushing was *claustrophobia*. The venue was a rabbit warren of dark corridors and unmarked doors. I'd be lucky to make it out alive.

You probably won't even see him.

And that would be just fine. It wasn't as if I was in the market for anyone who made me feel like he did. Fuck making my heart skip. That muscle in my chest was dead and buried, and it could fucking stay that way.

Lights out. Showtime. The band hit the stage, and I caught the lead singer's opening vocal in what I hoped was the first of many epic shots.

Hope. That four-letter word. Shooting bands was one of my favourite ways to earn a crust, but gigs like this, dark and smoky, were a fucker to photograph. The sensible side of me knew I'd be lucky to get ten decent shots out of every hundred, but that didn't stop the thrill in my veins that came with embracing the job I loved.

I took a few snaps of the band head-on, then changed my lens and stepped to the side, focussing on the bass player, who had a presence I wanted to capture. With her lustrous red hair and milky tattooed skin, this chick was entrancing. She owned the stage, and I got a little lost in her until a change in tempo roused me.

The band slid seamlessly from a stomping anthem into something gentler in cadence, and I moved on, shooting the stage from every possible angle. Then I headed upstairs to the balcony to get an aerial view. On my way, I took in the crowd and the electric atmosphere. I knew the band's drummer from the summers I'd spent in Porth Ewan, and dug the EPs he'd sent me over the past few years, but I'd never seen them live, which I regretted now that I saw how awesome they were. The grungy bass and funky guitars made me almost wish I'd left my camera at home. That I was rocking out in the mosh pit with the hard-core fans.

Then I caught the redheaded chick in a shot that made my night, and everything fell into place.

The gig flew by. I filled a memory card and was halfway through a second when a hand on my shoulder blasted my tunnel vision.

I jumped, half stumbling out of my crouch, and collided face-first with a lean, wood-scented chest.

"*Shit.*" And thank fuck for neck straps. I'd dropped cameras before, and there was nothing more depressing than seeing an expensive Canon smashed on the ground.

Strong hands steadied me. "Sorry, mate. Didn't mean to scare ya."

Kim. Of course it was. As his melodic brogue reached me, even over the pounding music, I let myself imagine that I'd recognise it anywhere.

I got my bearings, hoping I looked as unfazed as he seemed to be. "All right?"

He grinned and offered me a beer. "Cheeky one on the job?"

"Hell yeah." I took the bottle and downed half of it in one go. "Cheers. It's fucking boiling up here."

"Yeah, I thought you looked hot." Kim drank from a water bottle with a smirk that made me forget about the camera around my neck and the band tearing up the stage below. "And happy, which makes sense."

"Makes sense?"

"Aye-aye. No offence, but I could tell the jam shit wasn't your bag. Had you pegged for an artist . . . a designer, or a sculptor maybe, when I first saw you, but the camera fits. It suits you."

"Suits me?" In the back of my mind, I was aware how dense I sounded, but my ability to string a sentence together seemed to evaporate more with every second I stared at Kim. At his messy hair and warm eyes. At the artfully tatty T-shirt stretched across his chest. Dear God, he was something else.

Kim chuckled. "Trust me. I've been watching you dart about this place since I got here, and it's probably the coolest shit I've ever seen. Last photo I took, I chopped my pa's head off."

I didn't see how that made me cool, but I took the compliment. Coming from Kim, it felt more sincere than anything I'd heard in a while. "Trust *me*, there'll be plenty of shots where I've decapitated people. Shit happens."

Kim smiled, but said nothing as I refocussed and snapped the last few angles I'd had on my list. When I was done, I half expected him to be gone, but found him behind me again. "So this is what you do?" he asked.

"Some days." I reclaimed my now-warm beer and took a healthy swig. "When I'm lucky."

"What do you do the rest of the time?"

"Editing, some design work. Anything that keeps me out of trouble."

"Trouble? You don't look the type."

Kim leaned closer, eyebrow raised.

I absorbed the scent of fresh-cut wood, and covered the dizzying effect it had on me with a snort. "Tell that to my step-mum. Everyone always told her my brother Gaz would give her the most grief, but I smashed that shit out of the water."

"I'm intrigued."

"Yeah?" I studied Kim, tried to gauge if his bright eyes and open stance were really the flirtation I wanted them to be. "What do you want to know?"

"Everything."

Okay. My brain failed me for a moment. Most of my anecdotes involved heavy drinking and the hooliganism, but I had other stories too. Tales of being caught with my pants down by my elderly grandmother, exploring the anatomy of the summer help from the neighbouring farm. Did Kim seriously want to hear those?

The rational voice inside me said *no*, until Kim edged closer, his thigh touched mine and his wayward hair brushed my cheek.

The air shifted. "I've been watching you all night."

"Really?" I swallowed thickly. "What did you see?"

"Enough."

"Enough for what?"

"Enough to know that I want to see more."

I tightened my grip on my beer bottle. Felt the warmth of the glass seep into my palm. "Like what?"

Kim plucked the bottle from my hand and set it on a nearby ledge. *"Everything."*

We pushed our way through the crowded venue. Kim's hand was hot at the base of my spine, and I felt him behind me with every nerve in my body. It crossed my mind to make for the nearest exit, catch a cab back to my Porth Ewan flat, and screw his brains out in the comfort of my bedroom, but I couldn't wait.

I led him downstairs and backstage. Around us, the band's road crew were hard at work, packing up equipment and untangling wires, but they paid us no heed as we slipped past them to the storage rooms below the performance area. I tried one door, then another, and another, until I found the prop room I was looking for—the only room that locked from the inside.

Kim kicked the door shut behind us. We stared at each other. Above us, the thudding bass of the show's after-party kept tempo with the blood rushing in my ears. Then Kim moved—a blur in the dim light— pinned me against the door, and the surrounding noise dulled to a low roar.

It had been months since I'd kissed someone. I'd had a few fucks since my life had imploded, but they'd been just that —*fucks*—no kissing or lingering eye contact. No connection. Nothing like the heat that sluiced through me the moment Kim's lips touched mine.

I fell into his kiss with a crazed hunger that he matched with every clash of teeth and plundering swipe of his tongue. Lips, jaw, neck. I shoved my hand into his silk-soft hair and tugged as he bit down on my collarbone.

"Damn." I tipped my head back.

Kim pressed himself against me, his hard, sinuous muscles digging into my bones. "I've been thinking about this all day."

I couldn't deny I'd done the same. I slid my hands under his T-shirt and roamed the smooth skin of his back. "Yeah? What else did we do in your dirty daydreams?"

Kim dropped to his knees and unbuckled my belt. "This."

My head hit the door with a dull thud. Kim yanked my jeans down, then my boxers, and shot me an evil smirk as my dick sprang loose, giving away how much I wanted his mouth on me. "Do it," I whispered. "Show me."

Kim closed his lips around my cock and sucked me down deep. He moaned around me and met my gaze with a dark stare that made my knees tremble as I clenched my fists. Fuck, it felt good. I couldn't recall the last decent blowjob I'd had, and none in recent memory held a candle to what Kim was doing to me.

I groaned, glad I'd had the foresight to hustle him to a place no one but him would hear me. The last time I'd been down here had been to gather wooden farm animals for my brother Davey's A-level drama production. In a distant place in my mind, it felt comforting to know nothing had changed here in the decade since.

A shift in pace brought me back to the present. Kim had slowed his movements and tugged my balls, and now he pulled off with a wet pop. "I want to fuck you."

My heart raced. It had been a while since I'd last bottomed. Rich—my ex—had been an inflexible top, and I'd gone through a phase of rebellion when we'd finally split for good, fucking anyone who'd been willing. Cold and clinical—getting off, then getting gone. I'd sworn I'd never go back to how it had been with Rich . . . never give myself to anyone like that. Body, mind, soul, whatever. But the vow escaped my conscious thought as I fumbled for my wallet. I *wanted* Kim. Wanted him all over me, inside me, deep and brutal. I wanted him *now*.

I pushed a condom and a lube packet into his hands. "Do it."

"You sure?"

"Fuck yeah." In case he needed convincing, I turned, placed my palms flat on the door, and widened my stance. For an aching moment, nothing happened. Then I heard the zipper on Kim's jeans and the tear of the condom wrapper, and I closed my eyes.

Kim made short work of getting me ready. It might've been a while for me, but he seemed to sense that I didn't need a gentle touch. That I craved the burn and stretch of his dick inside me.

He withdrew his fingers and pressed the blunt head of his cock against me. My eyes watered. He felt big, really big, and my body resisted, fought him, until he slipped past the mutinous muscle and slid home, slow and smooth, like we'd done this before. Like my body fit his like a glove, the perfect balance of pleasure and pain.

"*Fuck.*" I panted out sharp breaths. Heat flooded my face and sweat trickled down my back. It *hurt*, but, fuck, it was good—better than good. I'd forgotten how the push and pull of a man's cock inside me could be so consuming.

Kim pressed in until he could go no further. Then he rubbed my back and squeezed my shoulder. "Okay?"

"Yeah." It came out as a strangled groan, but the sentiment reached Kim all the same. He dug his nails into the sensitive flesh above my hip bone, and withdrew enough so he could slam back in with a jarring thrust that drove the breath from my lungs.

He growled and did it again, and again, setting a rhythm that erased all coherent thought from my mind. The dusty storeroom and the noise from above faded away, and my world narrowed to the brutal dig of his cock, and his gravelled grunts and groans.

Shit, he was good at this. I almost wished that I could see him. That I could watch his muscles bunch and constrict, and absorb the snarl I imagined his full lips forming with every thrust of his hips. But there was something about getting fucked from behind, raw and rough, hands on the peeling paint of a door, or the cool concrete of an industrial wall. Something primal, and sordid, in all the right ways.

Shame it wasn't going to last long.

Kim leaned over me and bit my shoulder blade. I shivered through a groan, and the first stirrings of orgasm burned in my belly. I found my dick and matched Kim's movements as my eyes rolled, and my sweaty hand slipped on the door.

I gasped. "You're gonna make me come."

"Shit, yeah. Do it. I'm close."

Kim pulsed and swelled inside me. The sensation blew my mind, and my balls tightened to that painful point of thrilling agony, those dragged-out moments before coming when I was sure that I'd combust before I shot my load. "Harder."

"Jesus." Kim pulled on my hips and shoved my head down with his other hand, bending me in half. The change in angle led his cock to that magic bundle of nerves that made me shout, as I buried my face in the crook of my elbow and came like a motherfucking train.

"Fucking hell." I shuddered and spilled into my hand, distantly aware of Kim behind me, growling out a few choice words of his own, lost in the shot of warmth soothing me from the inside out, and the crashing rush of the hottest climax I'd had in years.

It seemed like I'd just blinked as Kim eased out of me and coaxed me upright. He kissed the back of my neck and smoothed my sweat-damped hair out of my eyes. "All right?"

I hummed, better than all right, but incapable of intelligible speech. Kim chuckled and fumbled around. Fabric touched my hand, my back, and my legs, cleaning me up, then he spun me and pressed his forehead to mine.

"*Your* daydreams next time, eh?"

CHAPTER
THREE

"Next time . . ."

Fuck's sake. If there was one thing worse than editing reams of photos, it was editing them when my mind was elsewhere. Like the weather, the lunch I'd forgotten to eat, or the crazy-hot fuck I'd had at the weekend.

Next time.

Yeah. Nice theory.

Shame Kim and I had stumbled out of the gig venue, dazed and awkward, without figuring when—or if—that would really happen. I'd been halfway home before I realised we hadn't exchanged numbers, an oversight that bothered me more than I cared to admit.

Irritated, I glared at my computer screen. In my distraction I'd thrown a random texture over the image I was working on, instead of reducing the background noise. I sighed and undid the action. The statuesque chick from The Mocking Horses was rocking the film grain, but it would probably take every trick in the book to make her look bad. This woman was *beautiful*.

I worked on the gig shots for most of the afternoon. The

redhead had captured my attention, but I'd be lying if I didn't admit that I spent most of my time scanning the crowd shots for Kim and his wild mop of hair. His lean shoulders and arresting smile. The venue had been dark and smoky, but Kim possessed a grin that brightened any room he walked into . . . in my head, at least. The only room I'd taken him into had been a fucking broom cupboard.

It was early evening by the time my phone pulled me out of my editing-induced stupor. I glanced at the screen, saw my stepmother staring back at me, and scowled. Fucking Gaz setting her up on FaceTime. There was no escaping her now. With that in mind, I accepted the call, since it was safer than risking her showing up on my doorstep.

And obviously she asked me if I was all right. She always did, and my answer was always the same.

"Course I am." I hauled myself off the sofa and stretched out the kinks in my spine. "Did you need me for something?"

"Dinner," she said. "Your brothers are coming. I thought it would be nice if you joined us too."

I rolled my eyes, glad I had my face turned away from the screen. Of course my darling brothers were home for dinner. They both lived in cottages on the bloody farm. It was only me, the perpetual black sheep, who stayed away. "I dunno. Do you mean tonight? I've got a load of work still to do."

"You can take a break, can't you? Come on, Jasper. We haven't seen you all week."

I didn't point out that I'd seen her for breakfast five days ago, and had spent the whole of my Saturday at that stupid crusty festival. Logic didn't work on my wonderful stepmother. If she wanted me home for dinner, I'd be home for dinner. It was easier that way. Besides, I hadn't looked in my fridge for days, preferring the company of my coffee machine and the bottle of Grey Goose I kept in my living room.

Thursday night was pie night on the farm, and now I thought about it, there wasn't much I wanted more.

Except a rematch with Kim.

"Jasper . . ."

I let my step-mum drown out the voice in my head and searched the detritus around me for some jeans. "All right, all right, I'm coming. I'll be there in a bit, okay?"

"Seven o'clock," she retorted. "Don't be late, or your dad will have you out on feed duty."

I *was* late, but somehow still the first of my siblings to arrive. Tardiness was in the Manning genes. The dogs met me in the yard, smothering me like they hadn't seen a human for months, and I found my stepmother in the kitchen, who wasn't much better.

"*Jasper.*" She squeezed the life out of me. "You're so pale. You look like you haven't seen the sun."

She was more right than she knew. Today had been the first day all week I'd crawled out of bed before 2 p.m, but she didn't need to know that. So what if I was a night owl? There was more to life than milking cows at the arse crack of dawn.

"I'm fine, ma." I wriggled out of her embrace and swiped a bit of bread from the counter. "Where are the others?"

Laura Manning stared me down a moment, before the oven timer distracted her. "Davey's up the fields with Dad, and Gary got caught up on the motorway. He said to start without him."

Gaz hadn't answered to "Gary" in years. I hid my smirk with another bit of bread. "What's he on the motorway for? Where's he been?"

"Sourcing furniture for the barn."

"Yeah?" For as long as I could remember, the biggest barn on the farm had been derelict, too vast and draughty for the small collection of animals my family kept alongside their arable operation, and too beat-up to store equipment of any value. Then Gaz had taken over the commercial side of the business and decided the barn would be the perfect venue for his latest harebrained scheme: an organic canteen, serving up the delights Laura and Davey's wife, Francesca, cooked up from surplus produce. I'd written off the pie-in-the-sky plans years ago, but recently, after a hundred false starts and terminal procrastination, things had begun to move and the barn had grown into something humans could inhabit. "What kind of furniture is he looking for?"

Laura shrugged, half-engrossed in her cooking. "He mentioned wicker, but you'd have to ask him. I'm just the kitchen skivvy."

"As if. We'd all perish without you, ma, but seriously? Wicker? What the fuck is he thinking?"

"Language, Jasper." Laura heaved a huge pie out of the oven and set it on the kitchen table. "And what's wrong with wicker? I thought it sounded nice."

"Yeah, if you're eighty-seven and have a conservatory built from curtain poles and PVA glue." Bloody wicker. Why didn't they get some polyester and Formica while they were at it?

"It's easily fixed," Laura said lightly. "Talk to your brother if you have ideas. You know he'd love to have you work with him."

"Yeah, maybe."

I left my vague answer hanging, but later, over dinner, my irritation with wicker-gate got the better of me, and I found myself beside Gaz, grilling him on his plans for interior design.

"Piss off, mate." Gaz shovelled mashed potato into his mouth and pointed his fork at me. "This ain't London. Folk round here don't want tiny candles and fancy bollocks."

"Who said anything about tea lights? I just think you should incorporate the aesthetic into the whole project. What's the point of marketing the food as organic and wholesome, then serving it up on a load of plastic crap?"

"What do you care?"

He had a point, but with Kim still fresh in my mind, I had an idea percolating. "What about some of that recycled stuff from the crusty-fest last weekend?"

Gaz eyed me like I was off my rocker. "Recycled stuff? Like what? Tables made from bog roll?"

"Stop being a twat. No, I mean like the stall in the back field. The one with all the stuff made from pallets."

"Didn't see it. I worked all day and didn't get the chance to swan around browsing."

I wanted to clobber him. There were four years between Gaz, Davey, and me, which meant we knew just how to wind each other up. "Fine. You're right. I *don't* care. Have it your way and dress the whole thing up like an eighties jumble sale."

Gaz sneered and went back to his pie. I glowered at the side of his head, then spent the rest of the evening ignoring him. Childish? Probably, but being at the farm had that effect on me. Crammed around the kitchen table, stuffing my face and up to my ears in the family business, it felt like I'd never been away.

I made my excuses around ten and headed out to my car. It wasn't that late and it would be hours before I crawled into my bed, but I'd had enough for one night. Davey called me a miserable bastard, but I didn't care. So what if I preferred my own company? At home, there was no one to piss me off, save my downstairs neighbours, who liked to have makeup sex as loudly as they tore lumps out of each other. Besides, I needed a fucking smoke.

"Jas! Wait up."

I turned, cigarette in hand. Gaz jogged out of the gloom, a conciliatory grin warming his face.

"Don't let ma catch you with that."

"Piss off." I rolled my eyes and lit up anyway. "What do you want?"

"Erm, I was thinking about apologising for winding you up about Kim, but I wouldn't mean it, so I'm not going to bother."

The casual mention of Kim caught me off guard. "You know him?"

"Only in passing. He works at that tattoo place, Blood Rush. Brix Lusmoore gave me his card when I told him we were scouting for furniture." Gaz pulled a small wooden disc from his back pocket. "Though Kim's stuff looks more like junk to me."

And that was the beauty of it. I held the disc up to the faint moonlight. Both sides had a simple logo carved into it, and the details I'd been ruminating on all week were inscribed around the edge: a name, an address, and eleven magic numbers.

"Thought you might like it."

I glanced back at Gaz. Somehow, I'd forgotten he was here. "Meaning?"

"Meaning I saw you chatting him up in the beer tent. That why you want me to use his furniture in the barn?"

"I never said you should use it. Just that your ideas were shite."

"Yeah, yeah. Listen, from what little I know of him, he seems like a nice bloke, and I was only joking about his work being junk. How about you give him a call, see if he can do us a quote? Might get yourself a reason to paint a smile on that ugly mug."

A facetious retort played on my tongue, but I bit it back as I considered Gaz's proposal. The address on the wooden disc was in town, not far from my flat. What was to stop me passing by, sticking my head in the door, and pretending I gave enough of a shit about the barn project to seek out his work?

Nothing and everything was the simple answer. Kim had been an awesome fuck, but that was about all I was good for these days. All I *wanted* to be good for. Getting close to people, close enough to bang them more than once, was overrated. Despite angsting over not grabbing Kim's details when I'd seen him, now that I had them, reality kicked in. No good ever came from returning to the scene of the crime—not even one as hot as my encounter with Kim.

I passed the disc back. "No, thanks, mate. Just stick to the wicker, eh? What's the worst that can happen?"

A week later, *of course* I found myself loitering outside the address I'd memorised from Kim's calling card. The exterior of the building was nondescript, but wood scented the cool breeze and I sensed Kim's presence. Felt it tickling my skin and warming my bones.

Twat.

I shook myself and braved a few steps forward. Outside the workshop, odds and sods of materials were stacked in haphazard piles. Pallets, obviously, and some old crates, and by the door a stack of battered aluminium. I studied the piled up sheets and tried to imagine what Kim might use them for. Nothing came to mind, but why would it? My creativity was limited to Photoshop, Lightroom, and pissing around on Illustrator. I couldn't build a fucking sandcastle.

Go inside.

Could not for the life of me fathom why that seemed so hard, but I left the aluminium behind and forced myself to wander into the workshop.

The *empty* workshop, until a lad popped up from behind a pile of corrugated iron. "All right, mate?"

"I'm looking for Kim," I said. "He around?"

The boy inclined his head to the left. "Upstairs. Go on up."

"Cheers." I headed for the steps at the back of the open-plan workshop. They led to a corridor, an office, and Kim, who was on the phone.

If he was surprised to see me, he hid it well. He muttered a hasty goodbye to whoever he was talking to and treated me to a grin that set off every facet of his devilishly handsome face. "Ain't you a sight for sore eyes? Wasn't sure I'd see you again."

"It's a small town," I hedged. "You'd have run into me eventually."

"That's what I've been hoping. Been kicking myself for not getting your number."

"That right?" My heart skipped a beat. I hadn't allowed myself to wonder if I'd been in Kim's thoughts as much as he'd been in mine. "Well, I'm here on business, as it goes."

Kim cocked a brow. "If you're after that pool table you were eying up at the festival, you're too late. I delivered it to some Ukrainian bird in Newquay last night."

A real pang of disappointment rippled through me. I had nowhere to put Kim's boat creation in my minimalist flat, but I mourned its loss. The photos I'd taken on my phone had done the piece no justice. "Actually, I was hoping to scope you out for a bigger project. Have you got time for a coffee?"

"Coffee?" Kim pulled a face and my stomach sank. I'd sought him out because I wanted to see him again, to *see* if the heady encounter I'd replayed in my mind—and the crazy-hot spark—had been real. But after a long, sleepless week, ruminating over Gaz's lunatic canteen plans, I'd set my heart on persuading Kim to come on board. His work was amazing, and I couldn't envisage the barn without it.

My mind raced. In all the ways I'd pictured this scene playing out, it hadn't occurred to me that Kim might refuse to hear my pitch. "Or . . . I could just quickly explain now, and—"

Kim cut me off with a deep chuckle. "Fuck that. Let's go for an ice cream."

Well, okay then. It was barely lunchtime, but who cared?

We left the workshop and shuffled across the road to the best ice cream shack in town. I bought the cones, and we found a quiet bench. We made small talk for a little while, skirting around the fact that the last time we'd seen each other, he'd fucked me against a storeroom door. Then Kim ditched our rubbish and pulled me back to the reason I'd given for tracking him down.

I filled him in, showing him photos of the barn, and then the new plans I'd sketched out to replace Gaz's wicker fiasco.

Kim studied them, gaze turning thoughtful. "It's a beautiful building."

I snorted. "You should've seen it six months ago: it was falling down. Had been for years until Gaz got a bee up his arse about it."

"Still, look at these beams. They're gorgeous." Kim swiped through a few more snaps. "You're right about the wicker, though. It's proper naff."

"Finally, a voice of reason."

"Yeah?" Kim grinned. "You the lone wolf in this?"

"Black sheep, actually. They wanted my input. Now I reckon they're sorry they asked."

Kim laughed and put his hand on my arm. "Families are like that. You'll never win. Now when are we going to fuck again?"

CHAPTER
FOUR

The day after our impromptu ice-cream date, as it turned out. Though it wasn't exactly how Kim sold his invitation for dinner at his place. Instead, he agreed to draw up some plans for the dining/lounge area of the barn, and feed me home-made curry while I looked them over. And when he asked me, with the tingle of his hand on my arm making my toes curl, it was the best offer I'd had in years.

Didn't stop me winding myself up all day leading up to it. Kim's company, naked and otherwise, was sorcerous. Hours passed in the blink of an eye, and every grin and gentle gesture felt amazing, but alone in my flat, pacing the living room, none of it seemed real. I'd been wrong about this shit before. *Really* fucking wrong. Why not now?

Evening fell, and I walked up the dirt track that led to the address he'd given me so nervous I wanted to puke.

Kim met me at the gate, lounging beneath a hand-painted sign.

I raised a brow. "Blackbeard's Junkyard? That sounds like the weirdest jumble sale ever."

"Yeah, yeah, I know. I didn't name the place, one of the others did."

"Others?"

"Yep." Kim opened the gate. "Come on. I'll show you."

I followed him onto what at first glance looked like a farm. Chickens pottering around a few veg patches my dad would be happy to call his own. A weathered shed and an out of context Harley Davidson leaning against a beat-up garage. All normal stuff, right? It took me a moment to realise what was missing.

"Where's your house?"

Kim grinned. "You'll see."

I took his word for it as he showed me around the land he called home, and yet amongst the random sheds, greenhouses, and workshops, I didn't spot anything remotely inhabitable. What I *did* see, though, was every contraption under the sun designed for eco living. Mini wind turbines and recycling bins. Compost heaps, and solar-powered showers—three of them.

"How many people live here?" I asked.

"Permanently?" Kim closed the outbuilding housing a small generator. "Ten, but others come and go. Since I've been here, the most we've had is twenty-one."

"Twenty-one? Where the fuck do you all sleep? Outside?"

Kim shrugged. "Sometimes, least we did over the summer. These days I sleep with the apples."

"Eh?"

"We sleep in the trees, Jas. Look."

I felt like a right knob when I finally saw the old Roma trailers nestled in the vast orchard at the back of what I was beginning to realise was some kind of commune. Eight in total, spaced far enough apart to ensure privacy, and they were just about the most wonderful things I'd ever seen.

"*Wow*. Those caravans are gorgeous. Which one's yours?"

"That one." Kim pointed to the most secluded trailer, beautifully painted and named—if the hand-carved sign nailed to the door was accurate—Kingfisher Cabin. "It's got its own bathroom, a log burner, and a little bit of lekky when I need it. Wanna see inside? There's an extension and a deck out the back."

"Fuck yeah." I followed Kim through the orchard and up the wooden steps of the decking that surrounded his trailer. He opened the door and my pulse quickened. We hadn't made it out of the gig—a public space—without screwing each other's brains out, and the current still simmering between us was so strong I trembled from it—on the inside, at least.

But it was impossible to feel anything but at home as I stepped into the cosy trailer. Rustic and warmed by the deep coloured rugs and throws that covered every surface, it was exactly as I'd expected it to be. I saw him everywhere—on the low squishy couch, at the beautiful wooden table. Stretched out in front of the log burner, naked, and—

"Jas?"

Kim touched my arm. I jumped. "Huh?"

"Are you hungry? I've got curry and some random veg bits from the garden."

My stomach answered for me, reminding me that I hadn't eaten since a bowl of cereal at arse o'clock the previous night . . . well, this morning, technically. As Kim moved to the trailer's tiny kitchen area and took the lid off a couple of pans, the idea of not eating whatever he was cooking was fucking laughable.

Curry and some random veg bits turned out to be lamb madras, and a cauliflower dhanzak I couldn't stop eating. "Wow. This is amazing."

Kim shrugged like it was nothing. "Not too hot, is it? I'm a bit of a spice freak."

"It's perfect. I spent my gap year travelling in India, and I've not had curry as good as this since."

"Really?" Kim's eyes lit up. "I'd love to go to India . . . Thailand too. Can't see it happening, though. Too old for that shit now."

"Bollocks. You can't be that much older than me."

"Who says I'm older than you?" Kim's lips turned up in a grin.

I wiped my mouth and regarded him in the twinkly light of the lantern-lit trailer, but his face revealed nothing about his age. His eyes held a wisdom that had led me to believe he'd a few years on me, but I wasn't so sure now. "I'm thirty-one."

"So am I."

Awkward. "Sorry. You just seem so chilled and sensible against the shambles of my own life."

Kim snorted. "Me and Mr Shambles are old friends. But you've got me curious now. What's so shambolic about you?"

"Everything." I scraped my plate clean and then pushed it away. "I was trouble from the day I was born."

"How so?"

I shrugged. "I told you the swingers' party story, right?"

"You did. Didn't sound like it defined you, though."

"It doesn't, but I guess it set the tone for the rest of my life. I've always been a pain in the arse. I reckon my dad knows he dodged a bullet when my mum took me back to London."

Kim said nothing, tipping the last of the rice onto his plate. When he looked at me again, his gaze was measured. "What did your brother tell you about me?"

"Gaz? Not much. Just that you work at the cool tattoo place on the seafront. I got the impression he didn't know you very well."

"He doesn't, but you know what this town is like. People talk."

"And what do people say about you?"

"The truth. That I'm a pisshead . . . an alcoholic. It ain't no secret."

"Oh." For the first time since I'd spotted my boyfriend and his wife across a crowded room, I was truly lost for words. "I thought you were going to say you were a freegan or some shit."

Kim laughed. "Would that have been worse?"

I considered it and nodded, still processing Kim's revelation and trying to match it with the composed man sitting beside me. "I fell asleep to a documentary on freegans once. Dreamt about Biffa bins for weeks."

"Fair enough. I'll take that as an assumption that raiding wheelie bins for my dinner would have been exponentially worse than drinking myself to death for most of my twenties."

I took a long sip of the lemon-laced water Kim had put on the table with the curry. It was obvious he was testing me—laying it all out to be sure I could handle it—before this, whatever it was, became something neither one of us wanted to give up. Did he do this with every new person he met? I hoped not. Whatever his past, he deserved better than that.

"I drink," I said. "Sometimes I drink a lot and get drunk. Is that going to be a problem for you?"

The roll of Kim's eyes was so minute there was every chance I'd imagined it. "Abstinence isn't avoidance."

Fair enough. I took my cue to shut the fuck up in the hope that he'd elaborate. In return, Kim leaned forward and brushed the pad of his thumb along my cheekbone. The touch was gentle, and unexpected, and so subtly erotic that a lump formed in my throat. I swallowed, my fingers itching to wrap around his wrist and tug him closer, so I could fuse my lips to his and put to bed any fear that our previous encounter had been a fluke. But he dropped his hand before I could break the thrall he had over me, and the moment passed. "How long have you been abstaining for?"

"A hundred and seventy-five days."

I did the maths. Kim had been dry less than six months. "So—"

"It's an ongoing thing," he said. "I haven't lost my mind on it for a while, but I have slipped a few times—more than a few."

I sat back in my seat and tried to imagine my life without the comforting burn of a shot of vodka, or the buzz of an ice-cold beer. "How long have you been in recovery for?"

"Four years, off and on. I'd been dry for eighteen months before I fucked up last."

"Was there a trigger?"

"For fucking up? Man, there's always a trigger, an excuse. That's what AA's for . . . to learn better ways of handling them."

I'd pictured AA as a place for old men—a last stop for the winos who lived in the shop doorways on Oxford Street. In my ignorant imagination, young addicts fried their brains on Mkat and got sent to cushy rehab centres. "Thank you for telling me. You didn't have to. I wouldn't have lost my shit if I'd found out later."

Kim smiled. "I believe you, but I don't like hiding it. It's not healthy for me. Besides, if I hadn't told you, someone else would have. You can't hide anything in Porth Ewan."

"Sounds like you've tried."

"Hasn't everyone? This place, though, it's something else, eh?"

I couldn't deny that. Porth Ewan hadn't been my home for a long time, if it ever truly had been, but the claustrophobic town possessed a certain magic, even if I did feel like I'd returned to it to die this time around. "Word on the street is that you're a tattoo artist as well as an epic carpenter. What came first?"

Kim shrugged. "I've been tattooing for as long as I can remember. Grew up doing it in my best mate's garage. But I'd been in AA three times before I realised my heart wasn't in it, at least, not in the way I'd thought it was."

Intrigued, I put my elbows on the table and leaned forward. "I've never met a tattooist who is anything less than obsessed with their work."

"Oh, I was—I am—but growing up, I was more into my mate than what we were doing."

Ah. The penny dropped. "Was he straight?"

"Brix? Fuck no, but we're like brothers, man. I saw that once I got out into the world and met other blokes, you know?"

Growing up in London, the world had been thrust upon me before I'd been truly ready for it, but Kim's tale was one I'd heard before. "How did you get into furniture making?"

"Through AA. My old sponsor was a chippie. He used to invite me down his workshop when I was having a bad day. Put a saw in my hand, and then a welder. I never looked back, 'cept when I fancy a skinful."

It sounded almost romantic, though I was willing to bet by the subtle tension in Kim's soft smile that it had been—and still was—a fucking rollercoaster. "One day at a time, eh?"

"Something like that. Anyway, enough about me. If you're not running for the hills, you wanna explain how you ended up back here when it's clearly the last place on earth you want to be?"

"Porth Ewan's not the last place I want to be."

"But?"

My turn to shrug. When had I become so transparent? "It's just not where I thought I'd end up. I had a good life in

London, and it was popping, you know? I could work three gigs a day if I wanted to. Back here I get three in a month if I'm lucky."

"Bet your quality of life is better, though. Brix looked like death when he moved home from the city. Took years of sea air to set him right."

"Brix Lusmoore? The bloke you were in love with?"

Kim rolled his eyes. "I was never in love with him. Brothers, remember?"

Yeah, yeah. I didn't know much about Porth Ewan's notorious Lusmoore clan, but I'd met Brix when my dad had bought some scruffy bald chickens from him, and the dude was almost as gorgeous as Kim.

Almost.

Not that being gorgeous made a man lovable, or worthy of the effort it took to bother. Fuck no. I'd learned that hard lesson, more than once, and I was done getting my heart burned.

Kim tapped my temple. "You're miles away. Don't be. Keep your shit to yourself if you want. I don't need to know anything about you, if you're happier that way. We can just fuck."

We can just fuck. God, the idea was tempting, but even as I turned in my seat and leaned closer to Kim, parting my lips in anticipation of his kiss, I knew it wouldn't be as simple as that. Couldn't be, because nothing ever was.

Kim's lips brushed mine, and the coherency required to give a shit evaporated. I kissed him back and let the thrill of his touch wash over me, eclipsing any sensibility I'd arrived with. Not that there'd been much, and before long, I found myself on my back with my legs hooked around Kim's waist.

I arched my spine, groaning as Kim wrestled with his belt buckle. "Hurry up."

"I'm trying." Kim finally loosened his belt enough for his jeans to drop down his slender thighs. "I'd kinda planned on getting you into my bed this time around, not fucking you at the kitchen table."

The fact that he'd planned to fuck me again sent shivers through me. I reclaimed my legs and let him shift us to a nearby rug. The contrast between the soft wool and the cool tabletop was electric. My heart sped up, and I watched, breathless, as Kim found a condom from who-the-hell-knew-where and rolled it on.

"Do you still have lube in your wallet?"

"Just spit on it."

"No way. That shit burns."

My lust-addled mind realised that his knowledge on the subject likely meant he was vers, and my cock throbbed so hard it hurt. I loved getting reamed until my mind was devoid of all else, but the thought of holding Kim's lean legs and sliding my dick inside him was bewitching.

But the need to have him inside *me* won out. I jutted my chin in the general direction of my discarded jeans. "Back pocket."

Kim retrieved the lube and slicked his dick. Then he nudged my legs apart with his knees and dropped a palm either side of my head, his cock pressing against me. "Damn. Didn't even get you naked."

It was true. Both of us were still wearing T-shirts and socks, but I was past caring. Kim slid home, and I groaned, almost undone by that single, devilish stroke. "*God.*"

"Right?" Kim flexed his hips. "It's bloody magic."

I couldn't think of a better word as Kim dug his fingers into my hips and fucked me. Lips caught in a snarl, I thrust my hips up to meet his fast-increasing pace, and it didn't take long for shit to get real.

Kim gripped my leg and pushed my thigh to my chest, snaking an arm under my shoulders to tug on my hair. His rough touch had me seeing stars, and I took myself in hand, pumping my dick to keep up with him. "Fuck, I'm gonna come."

And that was an understatement. I'd come like a train in the basement at the gig, my yells masked by the thumping bass above us, but this—being shunted across the floor of Kim's reclaimed trailer—was something else, something that would rattle the tin walls around us if I let it go.

Kim's hand slid from under me to grip my chin. His eyes were wild, his breathing sharp and scratchy. He fucked me faster, groaning with every brutal drive of his hips, and a beautiful flush coloured his cheeks. "I'm gonna come too."

Thank God. I watched, awed, as he fell apart, and then followed him, lost in the curve of his neck and his ragged cry. Wet warmth coated my stomach and hand, and heat pulsed inside me. I mourned the sensation lost to the condom, but as Kim dragged me up for a searing kiss, the reckless devil in my brain danced away. We kissed and kissed and *kissed*, until I had no real idea how long we'd been writhing on the floor. My dick hardened again, and I gasped in enough air to beg for round two. "Kim—"

The trailer door opened, letting in a warmish spring breeze that carried with it a sultry laugh and the distinctive floral scent of a woman.

"You started without me."

I'd never covered my cock so fast in my life, not even when my mum had caught me wanking in year ten. I wrenched my legs from Kim's grasp and scrambled to my knees, swiping my jeans from the floor.

I missed and toppled sideways. "*Shit*."

The woman chuckled again. "Don't get dressed on my account."

Oh hey, Red. I stared at the woman from the gig—the singer from The Mocking Horses, oblivious to Kim moving past me. In the flesh, she was as beautiful as the pictures I'd spent far too long editing: curvy and quirky, and covered in as much ink as Kim. I wanted to touch her, out of fascination more than attraction.

But Kim got there first. He grabbed her hand and started to pull her away. "Damn it, Lena. I told you I wasn't around tonight."

"That's why I'm here," Red—*Lena*, apparently—retorted. "To turn the burners off while you're out. I didn't realise you had company. I'm sorry."

She directed her last words at me. With my skin still

sheened with sweat—and other things—I didn't know quite how to respond. I wiped my stomach with my T-shirt and shrugged. "It's fine. I was—er—going, anyway."

"Jas—"

Kim reached for my hand before he seemed to remember he was already holding Red's, and something in the way he'd tangled his fingers in hers seemed significant. I tilted my head and regarded them, absorbing how their bodies had instinctively angled towards each other.

Shit. My stomach dropped. "You two are together."

It wasn't a question so much as stating the obvious. And the split-second silence that lacked the amused denial I'd subconsciously hoped for said more than whatever Kim opened his mouth to say.

I cut him off. "Don't. It's not like you told me anything different, is it?"

He hadn't. My assumptions were my own. I yanked my T-shirt over my head and searched for my shoes.

Kim's hand finally found my arm. "Don't go, Jas. It's not what you think."

Right. I forced a smile, struggling to keep my tone light as a brutal wave of disappointment washed over me. "It doesn't matter, mate. Honestly. It was just a shag."

Kim's hand fell away. I took my chance and pushed past him, spotting my shoes by the door. I stamped into them and made my escape, taking the wooden steps two at a time. The orchard had seemed beautiful when I'd arrived, the grass dappled with the setting sun as it filtered through the trees, but the canopy of leaves felt oppressive now, and I was drawn like a moth towards the fading daylight ahead.

"Jas! Wait."

Kim caught up with me on the dusty path that ran parallel to a field of strawberries I hadn't noticed on my way in. I kept walking, keeping my glare to myself. He didn't deserve it. Hadn't claimed to be gay, or single, or both. And, stupidly, I hadn't asked.

Stupid, because I'd played—and lost—this game before, though admittedly, this round had been lightning fast compared to the clusterfuck of my last serious relationship.

"It's okay." I reached the gate. "You don't have to explain."

"I wasn't going to. Seems to me that you don't want to listen." Kim's gaze was steady as he passed me an A4 envelope. "Figured I'd give you the drawings I did for you to take home. No reason we can't work together if it was just a shag, eh?"

I'd pretty much forgotten the original purpose of my visit had been to discuss the furniture plans for the barn renovation. The concept of upcycled tables and chairs seemed worlds apart from the chaos playing havoc with my insides.

Just a shag?

As Kim let go of the envelope and walked away, every instinct I had told me it was anything but.

I dragged myself back to my flat and hit the bottle, blocking the niggle of shame with swig after swig of Grey Goose. After hours of pacing, the couch called my name, and I wound up squint-glaring at the ceiling, dribble-ranting at myself for being a naïve twat.

Kim had told me no lies, but he hadn't told me the truth, either. My assumptions about his sexuality were out of place with everything I believed in, but he should've told me he had a missus . . . right? So what if she didn't seem to care that she'd pretty much caught him balls-deep in me? That was her prerogative. Me? I preferred to be kept in the loop. Surprises weren't my bag—every one that had ever been forced on me had been shite, and this one was no exception.

Fuck's sake. In the murky light of arse o'clock in the morning, the reality of how taken I'd been with Kim set it. I'd fucked my way around most of Hoxton before I'd admitted defeat and retreated to Porth Ewan, but I could barely remember a face, a scent, a sensation. I remembered every moment I'd spent naked with Kim. I remembered every moment I'd been in his presence, and fuelled by a bottle of vodka, the ridiculousness of my overblown sentiment set in. I'd known the bloke a fortnight, but the churning in my gut was ten times what it had been when my life in London had unravelled all those month ago.

What the actual fuck?

No sensible explanation came to mind, so I dragged myself from the couch and fetched my iPad from my office. A photography app was open, loaded with final RAW files that I really needed to sift through before I converted them, but I shut it down with barely a glance and opened Facebook instead. Kim didn't strike me as a social-media kind of guy, but what did I know?

It took me a while to track him down. I eventually found him tagged in a photo on the site for the tattoo studio—a photo of Lena wearing fuck-all clothes and baring her beautifully inked back. With considerable effort, I refrained from chucking the iPad across the room and snooped a little deeper. Kim's name appeared frequently on the studio's business page, but there wasn't much of him in the flesh. I clicked through to his personal page. His profile picture was of him with another man—Brix Lusmoore.

The tag confirmed it. I expected to find the rest of Kim's uploads awash with Lena, but she was absent, and his relationship status was blank.

Hmm.

I scrolled further down. His sexuality was listed as bi, no surprise, though I couldn't deny the flash of relief. And guilt. I'd judged Kim by someone else's piss-poor standards and had half expected him to be masquerading as a straight dude with a wife and two-point-four kids.

So you erased a whole slice of the spectrum? Including yourself?

Nice. The niggle of shame that I'd avoided by hitting the bottle finally kicked in. My insecurities weren't Kim's, or Lena's, whatever—*whoever* she was to him. They were mine, and were only still with me because I allowed them to be. I was a grown man, not a green teenager, and I'd fucked up the one thing—my family aside—that had brightened my life in Porth Ewan.

Kim likely thought I was a total wanker, and as I sloped off to bed to jack off and pass out, I reckoned he wasn't far wrong.

A few days later, the pleasurable ache at the base of my spine had faded, but the cloud of despair remained. I stayed off the booze—mostly—and worked myself into a Lightroom-induced migraine. When it had eased, and my fridge had reached a critical state of depletion, I admitted defeat and ran home to my stepmother, craving the comfort she'd always been so much better at giving than my own mum.

She didn't ask what had led me unshaven and bedraggled to her kitchen counter. Just dumped a dish of cauliflower cheese in front of me, and put the kettle on the stove. After plying me with obscene amounts of sweet tea, she asked the one question that could put me off the first hot meal I'd had in days.

"Did you get to speak to that carpenter man about the barn furniture?"

I pushed the baking dish away. "He's not a carpenter. He does welding and shit too, and tattooing."

"And?" Laura looked at me expectantly. "Tattooing isn't much good for our old barn, and for God's sake don't let your brothers get any more ghastly ink, but the welding sounds interesting. What did he have to say?"

I wondered if I'd called her in my sleep and told her of my plans to visit Kim at home. As luck—or not—would have it, the envelope Kim had pressed into my hand was in my camera bag, something I rarely left the house without.

With Laura at my shoulder, I spread the contents of the envelope out on the kitchen table. Sketches, mostly, inter- spersed with a couple of Polaroids of existing pieces I assumed Kim wanted to work from: snapshots of artfully rusted fishing equipment and seaside paraphernalia. The concept was a perfect blend of the farm's rural setting and the wild seas of Porth Ewan just beyond the gates.

I *loved* it, like I'd loved Kim's work from the start, and however much I'd embarrassed myself, that hadn't changed. If I could wrestle the rest of the design plans away from my hapless brother and negotiate a fair price from Kim, the barn could truly be something special. My imagination took over, and I pictured the rustic canteen I'd dreamed up when Gaz had first mentioned his harebrained idea. Laura and Co.'s food combined with Kim's chalk-white pallet tables and chairs . . . Damn, if I hadn't been so intent on mourning what had never been mine to begin with, I'd have been pretty fucking excited.

As it was, I let Laura's obvious delight seep into me and accepted one of her crush-to-the-bosom hugs.

"Ah, sweetie," she said. "It's so nice to have you here, but you're skin and bone. Won't you tell me what's wrong?"

My slim-ish frame had nothing on Kim's slender limbs, but my only answer was a shrug.

Laura clicked her teeth like I was five years old again and refusing to tell her where I'd last seen my missing shoe, and then she sighed. "I'll admit that I don't know your mother that well, but sometimes, you're just like her—so quick to speak your mind about everything except what matters."

"Is that your way of calling me an opinionated brat?"

"No, dear. Quite the opposite."

I didn't get it, but my best mystified scowl had no effect on Laura. She hugged me again, made more tea, and continued to study Kim's designs until my father joined us a little while later.

"Someone 'ere for you, lad."

"Me?" I barely glanced up, too engrossed in a set of chairs that looked like they belonged on a film set. "Not that bloke from the dairy is it?"

My dad glared. My sexuality had been embraced by the whole Manning clan with open arms, but shagging the milkman's son hadn't gone down well, especially when my dad had caught us in the barn in question. *"Dear Lord, Jasper. There's five bedrooms in the house. Have you no self-control?"*

Apparently not. "If it's not Carl, who is it?"

"See for yourself," my dad grumbled. "I'm having a brew."

Sighing, I tore myself away from Kim's mastery and drifted outside, my mind still on the barn. I had few friends in Porth Ewan outside of the ones I'd borrowed from Gaz and Davey, and part of me wondered if this was another of my father's attempts to coerce me into taking home one of the farm's stray cats—his lifelong mission.

Despite the fact that he'd been on my mind from the moment I'd met him, Kim was the last person I expected to see.

"Fuck. It's you. What are you doing here?"

Kim shrugged. "Found *me*, didn't you? Thought I'd return the favour." He kept his gaze on the chickens. "And I came to talk to your kin about the barn. I've just had some old dinghies dumped at the shop. I was considering making them into a couple of kitchen-island-type things, if you think they'd be interested? They could use them for display . . . serving counters, whatever."

The idea fit with the concept of bringing the outside in, but I couldn't deny that it wasn't what I'd hoped to hear from him. "You came to talk about the barn?"

Silence, then a wry grin warmed Kim's face. "I came to talk about the barn in the hope that you'd be here. That cool?"

It was beyond cool. I nodded and inclined my head behind me. "Do you want to come in? My step-mum bakes, so there's cake and shit."

"Actually, I'd like to see the barn, if that's okay? I rode my bike past this place every day of my childhood, but I've never passed your gates."

A crude joke played on my tongue. I swallowed it and gestured forward. "Come on, then. I'll show you around."

I gave Kim the grand tour of Belly Acre Farm—the animals, the fruit tunnels, the barley fields. The salad crop seemed to fascinate him. He stooped and fingered the pale leaves of the young round lettuces. "These are so much better than mine. Even the ones the slugs didn't get are crap."

"My dad's always had a way with greens. We lived off lettuce soup most summers to get rid of them."

"Yeah? Sounds delicious."

I pulled a face. "Six weeks of it wasn't."

Kim chuckled. "Think yourself lucky. My mum can't cook for shit. I grew up on tinned ravioli and crumpets."

"Are you close to your parents?"

Kim stood and stretched his spine. "Not really. They love me, they just don't get me."

"Outsider looking in?"

"Nah, it's not that. It's more they wish I was someone else . . . someone they understood."

"Straight and sober?"

Kim grimaced. "Straight and man enough to handle a few pints."

"Addiction doesn't make you weak."

"I know that now. It just took a while."

We started walking towards the barn. Our elbows bumped a few times and the urge to take his arm was strong. I didn't, though, and it struck me ridiculous that I'd had the patronising audacity to tell an alcoholic what his addiction meant. "Sorry."

Kim slanted a glance at me. "What for?"

"Anything. Everything. There's bound to be something. I tend to speak—and act—before my tiny brain engages. I'm that bloke who's forever cringing and apologising, you know?"

"I don't know you yet." Kim's gaze swept the horizon before it landed on me. "But I'd like to, and believe me, I ain't ever known anyone perfect. Flaws make us human."

Coming from me, the sentiment would've sounded like a Waitrose fortune cookie. From Kim, it was poetic and made me want to forget his girlfriend and drag him into the nearest outbuilding.

But I couldn't forget Red, and as the barn appeared in front of us, I knew that, sooner or later, the time to pretend I could would be over.

I led Kim inside the barn. It was a mess of dust and tarpaulin, but the potential of the space was plain to see. At the back, Gaz and his builder mate—Bob, no joke—had begun to install the kitchen, and the roof was finally secure and leak-free.

"This place is awesome," Kim said.

"It's on its way," I countered. "I keep changing my mind about whether we'll pull it off, though."

"Why's that? Apart from the décor, you seem to have a clear vision of what you want."

I shrugged. "The more I think about it, the more I wonder if I'm looking at it the wrong way. Like a Londoner, perhaps? Maybe Gaz does know best."

"He was wrong about the wicker."

"True, but what about the rest of it? I was thinking last night about a shoot I did last year for a company who are, like, the fucking masters of concept restaurants. Seriously, they open a new place every year, and each one is so crazy-amazing the whole city stops and takes notice."

"And that's what you want to do here?"

"No." I shook my head. "I thought we should, for a while,

but I was wrong. Gaz and Davey—all my family—have dedicated their whole lives to this. That should speak for itself."

Kim smiled. "It is the Porth Ewan way."

His wisdom gave me a clarity I'd been lacking. I shelved the fancy plans I'd drawn up in my head and gazed around the barn, again imagining it filled with Kim's original furniture, and the scents of a lifetime of my family's best-loved recipes. Kim was right: this *was* Porth Ewan, and the barn had a soul that couldn't be moulded to fit whatever hipster lunacy I'd brought home from the city.

That settled, I couldn't ignore the elephant in the room any longer. I drifted to a stray hay bale that seemed to keep finding its way back into the barn and sat down, absorbing the prickly texture. "So . . ."

"So . . ."

Kim trailed to a stop in front of me, his hands loosely at his sides, like he had these awkward conversations all the time. Perhaps he did. I regarded him through my fingers as I shielded my eyes from the stream of sunlight filtering through one of the new windows Gaz had installed. "Tell me about Red."

"Red?"

"Lena. Sorry. I called her Red when I was shooting her at the gig."

"And you still do?"

"Well, not to her face, obviously."

Kim smirked a little. "Shame. I think she'd like that."

"You'd know, I suppose."

Kim's humour faded. "I never lied to you, but for what it's worth, I'm sorry."

That Kim hadn't lied to me, I couldn't deny, and the first time we'd fucked at the gig—at *Red's* gig—we hadn't exactly stopped to ask each other any pertinent questions, like *Any chance your girlfriend is gonna walk in on us?* And, as my drunken internet stalking had made me realise, it was actually Kim who was due an apology. "I'm sorry too. I made assumptions I shouldn't have."

"Assumptions about what?"

I shrugged. "The usual crap—that where you're putting your dick at a particular moment defines your whole identity. I'm fucking mortified that it was in me to be something I've spent my whole life fighting."

Kim sat down beside me, stretching his long, jean-clad legs out in front of him. "So you thought I was gay? And single?"

"It's not like I bothered to ask, but yes. I kinda let myself assume."

"And now you think I'm straight and taken."

"Not quite." I averted my gaze, unwilling to admit to my Facebook spying. "How wrong was I?"

Kim shifted, perhaps knowing my fascination with him would force me to look at him. "Dude, I'm pansexual as fuck— I ain't ever been straight. And I've been single for more months."

I let what I'd already known wash over me and absorbed the rest. "You're single?"

"Yup."

"But—" *But what?* How could he be single when the heat between him and Red had just about burned my retinas? I sighed. "There's something between you and her, but she didn't seem to mind catching you with me. Friends with benefits? Not that you have to explain yourself to me, or anything. I mean—"

"Jas, it's fine. I didn't come here to bullshit you."

"Thought you came to look at the barn?"

"Are you going to let me speak?"

I pursed my lips and waved my hand. Kim looked like he

might laugh, but he didn't. His gaze remained fixed on mine as he leaned back and folded his hands behind his head. "Me and Lena go *back*. We met at an ink convention in Bristol a decade ago. She's kinda my soul mate, but we ain't together now, and that isn't going to change."

"You split up?"

"A while ago. I love her to bits, but there's more out there for both of us."

"But you still have sex."

It wasn't a question, but Kim nodded anyway. "Not often, just when she's down these parts and we're both single, or with folk who like to play too. She lives in Bristol, when she's not on the road with TMH. She's only in Porth Ewan for a few weeks while they tour Devon and Cornwall, then she's off to the States."

"*. . . with folk who like to play too.*"

The way Kim's mellow voice wrapped around every word made me shiver in ways my brothers' local accents never had. I rubbed my arms and tried to make sense of the whirling dervish in my mind. Kim wasn't with Red after all, but what did that mean? As I stared at him, I suddenly realised that I had no clue. The idea that he'd cheated on Red had made me sick to my stomach, but the knowledge that he hadn't—that he'd simply branched out from his usual brand of orgy— Jesus Christ. I didn't know whether to be turned on as hell, or fucking terrified.

Either way, I was grateful for his honesty, even if it did mean confronting the fact that my so-called liberal self was actually a judgemental bastard. "I don't know what to say."

"So don't say anything. I'm not asking for your approval."

Of course he wasn't. And why the hell should he? I shook my head, as much at myself as at him. "What really split you and Red up? Was it the drink?"

"It didn't help." Kim dropped his arms and leaned forward, losing some of his nonchalance. "I hit rock-bottom, more than once, and I think that's why she stayed with me so long. It took us both a while to believe I'd survive without her."

"But you manage, eh?"

"Just about. Brix coming home helped for a while—before the drink took over again. Life can get pretty lonely around here when you're the only bloke who likes cock."

I snorted. "You can't be the only one."

"Course I'm not. It just felt like it when Brix left all them years ago, and I found myself bereft enough to go looking for mates on the sauce."

"I'm glad you're not lonely anymore."

"Me too."

I chewed on my lip, my teeth gnawing at the chapped skin, a bad habit I'd developed in the throes of a mammoth photo-edit many years ago. The metallic taste of blood filled my mouth, and I welcomed it, glad of the distraction.

Emo, much?

Kim rescued my bottom lip with a swipe of his thumb. "I take it from your silence that you're not interested in hooking up again? Get to know each other a little better?"

Not interested? *God*, I was interested—too fucking interested, but after years of following my heart, my dick, and every other part of my anatomy except my brain, for once, common sense kicked in. "I'd love to get to know you better, but I haven't got the head space for anything more. I just got out of a shit relationship and—"

"Still reeling, eh?"

"Something like that." And that was putting it mildly. My own bisexuality meant the idea of Kim and Red together was hotter than I cared to admit, but I'd learned the hard way that crowded relationships brought nothing but trouble and heartache.

Kim smiled. "Fair enough. Can't blame me for asking, though. I really like you, Jas, and I was looking forward to seeing your work."

"That can still happen if you've got room for a mildly alcoholic, emotionally malfunctioning friend in your life."

My bad joke was out before I remembered I'd picked the wrong audience for my lousy brand of humour, but Kim's grin remained.

"I've always got time for my friends. You've got my number. Give me a call sometime."

He unfolded his lean frame from the hay bale and stood. I thought for a moment that he might say more, but he didn't. He put his hand on my shoulder, squeezing gently enough to set my bones on fire, then turned away, disappearing through the barn doors and down the grassy path that led to the main road.

I watched him go, entranced as ever by his slim shoulders and loping stride. It seemed like the end of the world when he disappeared. After all, I'd spent every summer in Porth Ewan and never crossed his path. If the barn didn't come together, chances were I'd never see him again.

CHAPTER
SEVEN

In the week that followed Kim's visit to the farm, he called my dad and committed to furnishing the barn while I wallowed in a pit of introspection. And then, as random deliveries of tables and chairs started arriving at the farm every few days, after years of not knowing he existed, I saw him *everywhere*: the shops, the bank—the pub, of all places.

I even ran into him at Truro train station on my way back to London to tie up some loose ends.

"You stalking me?"

His tone was light, his grin playful, but after a fortnight of trying to ignore how ridiculous his sudden presence in my world made me feel, I wasn't in the mood. Or, rather, I wasn't in the mood for trudging up to London to scrape together the remnants of the life I'd left behind, but the semantics didn't matter. All I knew was the longer he stood in front of me, the more likely it was that I'd bite his beautiful head off.

I sidestepped him, forcing a grin of my own. "Not my fault you're everywhere I go, is it? Who's the stalker?"

"Today? Technically, it's you, as I was here first." Kim

caught my arm. "What's the matter? You look like you're shitting a fridge."

Charming. I stopped and tried to gather the enthusiasm to reclaim my arm, but it was a tough ask as Kim's scorching hold seeped into me, threatening the bleak mood I'd woken up with that morning. "I'm fine. Just got a train to catch. What are you doing here?"

"I sent one of my guys to Edinburgh with a bunch of aluminium crockery sets for a gastro-pub."

"Edinburgh? That's some distance to go to deliver some plates. You couldn't post them?"

"I could've, but Corey's nanna lives up there. Might as well let him go and save my tax bill, eh?"

Couldn't argue with that. How many hours had I lost to pouring over my own accounts and wishing I'd figured out better ways to spend my money? "Anyway..."

I started to move off, assuming Kim would let me go, but he didn't. His grip on my arm tightened, and he pulled me back, turning me so I was facing him. "Seriously, what's the matter? Is something wrong?"

"Wrong? Nah." I shook my head, for some reason unable to look him square in the eyes. "Just got some shit to sort out."

"Bad shit?"

"Not bad in the tragic sense, but it's pretty fucked up." That was one way of putting it, but I didn't feel like explaining it, even now, months after the event.

Shame Kim hadn't picked up the unwritten Manning rule that reticence was a sign to leave me the fuck alone. He put his arm around me and stared up at the big screens. "What train are you getting?"

"The midday one."

"To London?"

"Yeah."

"It doesn't leave for fifteen minutes. I'll wait with you, if you like?"

For all my desire to wallow in a pit of solitary self-pity, I couldn't bring myself to refuse. We drifted to the northbound platform and sat on the grey metal benches. Kim eyed my twisting hands. "No bags. Day trip?"

"Hope so. I'm completing the sale of my flat tomorrow. Just got to sign some papers and pick up a few bits I left behind."

"Oh. Where's the flat? Anywhere nice?"

"Hoxton, so depends what you mean by *nice*. You don't strike me as the type of guy who appreciates grand-scale gentrification."

Kim pulled a face. "Charging people eight quid for a sarnie and all that hipster crap? No, thanks. Calum says the studio would make three times the profit if we set up shop in the big smoke, but we'd all be fucking miserable, and I reckon he's right."

"Probably. I'm a city boy, but those summers on the farm were the happiest I'd ever been."

"You're not happy now?"

"Is anyone?"

Kim said nothing. I uncrossed my legs and my knee brushed his. He flinched and stared at me, his expression unreadable. Had he felt it too? The jolt of energy that seemed to grow in intensity every time we touched?

And what the hell was he seeing in my face as I gazed back at him, lost in his scruffy jaw, chiselled cheekbones, and bottomless eyes? Could he tell how much I still wanted him? That I'd spent two weeks cursing myself for pushing him away, even though I knew it was the best thing for everyone?

"I could come with you," he said suddenly. "To London, I mean. Moral support. Company. Whatever."

"Aren't you busy?"

"Not today. Seeing Corey onto the train was the last thing on my list."

Kim didn't strike me as a lazy guy, and it was barely lunchtime. I dreaded to think how much he'd achieved in the time it had taken me to drag my arse out of bed and to the train station. "I can't ask you to come with me. Apart from anything else, it will be boring as hell. I'm just going to the flat, and then the estate agents."

"Won't take long, then, eh?"

"I doubt it."

"That's settled, then, cos whatever's put that cloud on your face, Jas, there ain't no reason for you to face it alone."

Kim bought a ticket on the train, and we settled into a carriage towards the back. Two seats, together, with no one around us. To my shame, I dozed off almost immediately, worn out by a long night of putting the finishing touches to the images I'd shot of Red's band, and then only a few snatched hours of restless sleep where my dreams had flitted between her, Kim, and the clusterfuck of heartbreak I'd left in London.

I woke with a jump somewhere near Bath, my cheek mushed against Kim's shoulder.

"Shit." I sat up and wiped my mouth. "Sorry. I'm a bugger for passing out on the train. I've ended up in Coventry before now."

Kim chuckled, keeping his gaze on the iPad he was drawing on. "Lucky Coventry. I got real bad travel sickness until a few years ago. Could barely ride an escalator without chunning."

"Nice."

"Not really. My dad is a fisherman. Drove him half mad that I was such a pansy out on the water."

There was no malice in Kim's tone, no bitterness. "I'm bi too, in case you were wondering. Most days, anyway."

He looked up from his work. "Yeah? How's that working out for you? Ever wish you were one or the other?"

"Not often. You?"

Kim shaded a petal on the rose sketch he was working on. "I'm cool with it, most of the time. It's hard, though. I've felt guilty in the past for liking blokes when I've been with a woman, and the other way around. But then I met Lena, and it didn't matter anymore. We both liked everything, so there were no boundaries."

"Free love and all that jazz?"

"Something like that." Kim sighed and turned his iPad off, tucking the stylus pen into the side of the case. "Look, I'm not incapable of being faithful because Lena and I chose to have an open relationship, if that's what you're thinking. And it didn't make us love each other any less. It's—it *was* just *different*, and for a long time, I was as happy as I could be with all the other bullshit I was dealing with."

"I don't think you're incapable of being faithful. And I come from a family of swingers, remember? It's just—" *Just what?* What exactly was I trying to explain here? That Kim's lingering relationship with Red was irrelevant? Because it was *me* who was emotionally broken? *Me* who'd closed off my heart from the possibility of ever loving anyone ever again?

"Jas."

I blinked. "What?"

Kim tilted his head. "I've never seen you like this. You're usually so . . . I dunno, fucking poised, and together. What's up? You don't want to sell the flat?"

How he knew the sale of my flat and my ramblings on

sexuality were connected, I'd never know. Letting loose a coarse breath, I plucked his iPad from his hands and raised an eyebrow, silently asking his permission to swipe through his sketches.

Kim nodded and leaned over to tap in his passcode. "There's a couple of folders on there. Enough to keep you busy for a while."

Perhaps I can love him after all. But as the errant thought crossed my mind, the train rumbled into Swindon, reminding me that only Reading stood between me and the city I'd sworn I'd never go back to. I opened a sketch of an old-school anchor-and-rope tattoo, similar to the one I'd seen on Kim's chest. The design was classically flawless, and for the umpteenth time since I'd met him, Kim's talent blew me away. *I don't deserve him.* "I've cheated on every partner I've ever had."

"That so?"

"Yep." I swiped through the pages of tattoo designs. "All but one. Bet you can guess that karma caught up with me, eh?"

"It don't always happen, but when it does, it's good for us. It's how we learn, how we grow."

"Or how we realise what we deserve."

"I don't believe that." Kim nudged me until I looked at him. "Fucking up doesn't mean we deserve to be hurt."

"Kim, I was an arsehole. Shit, I can't even explain it. Different girl every week. Blokes on the side. More girls. I wasn't a liar, but I think that made it worse, because I just didn't care. Drugs, booze, sex, it was all the same, you know?"

Kim hummed. "They often come together. Makes it hard to know what to quit first."

"Well, I quit it all when I found something—someone—who turned my life upside down."

"Ah, you fell in love?"

"God, yeah. Hard, like a motherfucker."

"Bloke or girl?"

"Bloke, which knocked me off my feet all over again."

"Why?"

I shrugged. "Because all the gay guys I knew up until that point were doing the same as me—fucking their way around Hoxton. No strings. No commitments. I guess I kind of assumed that's all there was for them . . . for *me*. And then I met Rich."

"The love of your life?"

"I thought so for a while. Four years, in fact."

"That is a while."

"Especially when you're wasting your fucking time."

I tried to keep the bitterness out of my voice. Failed, and the sympathy in Kim's kind eyes was hard to take. I preferred it when he gazed at me like I was the first naked man he'd ever seen. Which wasn't going happen again, right? Because I'd told him I just wanted to be friends.

Kim nudged me. "Tell me the punch line. Did he cheat on you?"

"Worse. He was cheating on someone else to be with me."

Kim winced. "Wife?"

"Wife, two-point-four kids, the whole shebang. And when I look back on it now, it's so fucking obvious. Shit, when I eventually found out, he'd been living a double life for our entire relationship—half the week with me at our flat, the rest of it in Northampton with his real family—"

I broke off as it occurred to me that this was the first time I'd told my tale of woe to anyone who wasn't one of the handful of faceless dudes I'd fucked in the weeks of drunken malaise that had followed Rich's revelation. And I was telling Kim on the train back to the scene of the crime, no less. *Jesus.*

"Go on." He nudged me again.

I took a deep breath. "I caught him red-handed. A client invited me to a book launch close to where Rich was living with his wife. I never bothered to tell him I was going, because he was working away, like he always did on Thursdays. Which I guess worked out for the best in the end, because if I'd told him I was going, I'd never have walked into the event to catch him breaking bread with his wife, his kids, and my big new client who just so happened to be his brother-in-law."

"Ouch."

I nodded. "Yep. I lost my life with him and a six-month contract that day. I care more about the contract now, but at the time it felt like the end of the world."

"I s'pose it was, in a way. The world as you knew it, at any rate."

"Yeah."

I'd run out of steam, and as luck would have it, the train pulled into Paddington at that moment, a mere four and a half hours after we'd left Truro. I stood and squeezed past Kim's legs, trying not to gawp as he unfolded his long frame, arching his swan-like neck to stretch out the kinks.

"How far is it to Hoxton from here?" he asked. "I've never been."

I navigated the jostling crowds until we were safely off the train. "It's forty-five minutes on the tube—here to Oxford Circus, then Kings Cross to Old Street. You don't know London at all?"

"Only where Brix lived, and even then I didn't visit that often."

"You're not missing a lot."

"No? Then why did it take you your whole life to leave?"

I didn't have an answer to that. Instead, I led Kim underground and onto the first of three trains that would eventually take us to Hoxton. Tube journeys were quiet by nature—it was the London way. Neither of us spoke much, and the silence was almost as comforting as Kim's presence beside me, and before I knew it, we were in Hoxton and outside the tidy garden flat I'd once called home.

Kim peered through the gate. "This is nice."

"It was, until I kinda trashed the place before I left."

"Understandable. Did it fuck up the sale?"

"No idea. I left the estate agents to deal with it. I haven't been back since the beginning of summer."

"Got keys?"

The Eiffel Tower key ring in my pocket suddenly felt like a brick. I retrieved it and dangled it on two fingers like it had been to Chernobyl and back. They were *Rich's* keys. I'd lost mine on a drunken night out in Farringdon and had borrowed his the week before I'd caught him basking in familial bliss with someone else. I'd hidden them in a plant pot when I'd moved into my Porth Ewan apartment, buried them, like their absence would take everything else with it. Out of sight, out of mind.

"Come on." Kim snagged the keys and reached across me to open the garden gate. "You don't want to be here, I get that, so let's get inside, get shit done, and piss off home."

I drifted after him to the front door. "You're starting to sound like my handler."

"Do you need handling?"

I cringed as Kim unlocked the flat's front door, picturing the mess I'd left it in. "Maybe."

But my apprehension proved unwarranted. The estate agents had done their job and gutted the place of any sign of my drunken tantrums. All that remained was a pile of broken furniture in the back bedroom, and a box of photographs some kind soul had been thoughtful enough to save.

I ignored the photos and glared at the smashed bookcase.

"I don't give a fuck about most of it, but I loved this bookcase. It was the first piece of grown-up furniture I ever bought."

Kim regarded the pile of splintered wood. "That's some serious rage, man. Did you do that to everything you owned?"

"Pretty much. I was blackout drunk at the time, and you probably know how that ends."

"My vibe was more drinking myself into a coma until this right here"—Kim gestured at the bookcase—"was about all that was left of me."

I swallowed thickly. Kim was so calm and poised that it was hard to imagine him as anything else. "I have so much respect for you."

"Why? I haven't done anything special. I'm just surviving." Kim moved past me to the window and gazed out at the Hoxton streets. "It's so busy here. Porth Ewan gets a bit crazy in the summer, but it never seems this . . . frantic. I feel stressed just watching these people."

I joined him at the window. "I guess that explains why visiting Porth Ewan always felt like crossing into Narnia."

Kim snorted. "Maybe. You think you'll stay?"

A few weeks ago, my answer would've been a solid *fuck no*. But standing in the barren wreckage of my old life with Kim by my side, nothing felt *solid*. Especially my heart. All I knew for certain was that I'd never come back to London.

With a sigh, I turned away, eying the box of photographs I really couldn't afford to ignore. God knew what was in it. The possibilities ranged from nudes of Rich to the lifestyle shots of a bowl of tomatoes I'd once done for a food magazine, and with any luck, the vintage images of the barn back in Porth Ewan, taken by the old owners sometime in the fifties.

I left Kim at the window and braved the box. As luck would have it, Rich's nudes were the first thing I put my hands on. With a grimace, I tossed them over my shoulder without looking at them, knowing that Kim would retrieve them. Though why I wanted him to see my douchebag ex in all his naked glory, I had no idea. Rich might've turned out to be a nuclear-grade arsehole, but he had a hell of a body—thickset and strong, sculpted muscles in all the right places. I'd never been so attracted to someone until...

Until I'd met Kim.

Damn. Despite my preoccupation with my self-pity party, I couldn't deny that Kim entranced me far more than Rich ever had, physically or otherwise. Hindsight was a wonderful thing.

"This is your ex?"

I glanced over my shoulder. "Don't be fooled by his baby face. He's fucking ruthless."

"Banker?"

"Wanker, actually, but yeah. He works in the city."

"Do you miss him?"

It was a question I'd asked myself a lot until I'd met Kim, and I still wasn't altogether sure of my answer. "I miss the company—as sporadic as it was—and the sex, but I don't think I miss him. Even without the clichéd double-life bullshit, he was a bit of a prick."

"You feel free without him?"

I shrugged. "Some days. Still hurts, though. Bastard broke my heart."

Kim came up behind me and peered over my shoulder. His hands were empty, but I didn't ask what he'd done with Rich's nudes. Didn't care. How could I when Kim was standing so close to me, the warmth of him making my skin tingle?

"Why have you got pictures of fairy dust?" he asked.

I picked up the images he was pointing at. "That's not fairy dust, it's sand shot with a macro lens."

"Seriously?"

Kim plucked a photograph from my hands and held it up to the light. His puzzled frown would've been comical if it hadn't been so endearing. "Why is it purple?"

"Because it *is* purple, at least that handful of grains was. Sand is a weird and wonderful thing if you look closely."

"And you have to care enough to look, eh?"

Kim didn't seem to expect an answer to that loaded question either, so I passed him the rest of the sand series and returned to sifting through the box. The old barn images were at the bottom, stuffed into a ripped brown envelope. I spread them out on the floor and snapped a few shots of them with my phone to send to Gaz. Hopefully, we could frame some of them and display them in the refurbished barn. I glanced at Kim. "Don't suppose you make picture frames, do you?"

"I can make anything if I've got the right materials." He appeared at my side. "What have you got in mind?"

"These." I nodded at the barn images. "I'd like to keep as much history in the barn as we can."

"Good job you got a pile of unused wood over there then, innit?"

I followed Kim's amused gaze to the smashed-up bookcase. "You can do something with that mess?"

"It's not a mess, Jas. It's a transition to a new life." Kim ambled over to the bookcase and produced a foldaway sack from the bag he'd brought with him. "See these bits here? 'Bout a foot long, I reckon. Do the trick nicely."

He started gathering lengths of splintered wood, while I stared at him like he'd suggested we collect kryptonite from the moon. He'd half filled the sack by the time I returned to the real world.

I didn't go and help him, though. How could I when the sunlight streaming through the large Victorian windows was hitting him so beautifully? My fingers itched for my camera, but for once I'd left my precious Canon at home. I pulled my iPhone out, loaded the app that allowed me to shoot in RAW, and snapped a few experimental shots.

Kim rolled his eyes. "Always working, eh?"

"Says you."

"Touché, I'm going to run out of wood to pick up in a minute, though. Want me to slow down?"

That he was so willing to humour me made me want to jump his bones. "No, just carry on. The sunlight behind you is perfect. Don't suppose you fancy taking your top off, do you? Ink and white walls are a fetish of mine."

Kim's only answer was a roguish wink as he set his wood-filled sack aside and pulled his Sheelanagig T-shirt over his head. He tossed it in my direction and turned around, showing me his lean, inked back in all its glory. And glorious it was. I snapped away, stepping closer with every shot, cursing the fact that I'd always been too busy getting off to take in how fucking stunning he was naked: his slender bones and sinewy muscles, his flawless skin. I wanted to take a thousand pictures of him—to already *have* a thousand pictures of him. I wanted to touch him, to press my face between his shoulder blades and breathe him in.

I *wanted* to sink my teeth into his neck.

So. Fucking. Much.

I settled for a quickened pulse as Kim unbuckled his belt. I'd never noticed what underwear he wore—and now I knew why. Because there was no underwear, not today, at least, only a narrowing trail of dark hair that led to the one thing I *definitely* recalled.

Swallowing, I snapped his skilled hands as they pushed his jeans down his hips, stopping short of what I wanted to see most. Camera forgotten, I dropped my phone in the box of photographs and stepped into Kim's personal space. My hands covered his, shoving his jeans down those final few inches, and our lips met in the kind of kiss that made me wonder what we'd been doing all day when we could've been doing this.

I pushed him against the wall, absorbing his low groan, and revelled in the way he fell slack in my arms. His cock dug into my stomach. I broke away only long enough to pull my T-shirt over my head, and then I dropped to my knees and took his dick into my mouth with a slow, wet, slide of my tongue.

"Jesus." Kim's head hit the wall with a dull thump. His legs quivered, and for the first time since I'd met him, his composure slipped. "Fuck, God, *yeah*."

I grinned at his incoherency and fumbled for my wallet and the single condom and sachet of lube that remained in it. Thank fuck, because I don't know what I would've done if yanking Kim to the floor and riding his dick had been off the table.

Supplies retrieved, I tried to find the willpower to release his cock from my mouth—a tough ask as his every sound and shudder travelled through me. I tore at my own belt buckle, seeking friction, and dragged my teeth along Kim's dick until he growled and pulled my hair, thrusting into my mouth, scraping the back of my throat.

"What do you want, Jas? You want me to fuck you right here? Screw all the bad memories out of you?"

It could never be so simple, but screwing Kim on the hard-wood floor of the home I'd shared with Rich was *going* to happen. Besides, Rich was the last thing on my mind as we stripped away our remaining clothes.

Kim lay back on the distressed floorboards, naked and beautiful, his inked skin too perfect for me to resist running my tongue over his chest and biting down as he groaned beneath me, deep and low.

"*Jas.*" His fingers dug into my hips, and I took the bruising touch as my cue to get a move on.

Biting my lip, I sank down on Kim's dick, paying heed to a subconscious plan to take it slow, ease him in. But my body and my brain didn't seem to be connected, and the moment he pierced me, all bets were off. I ground down hard, pressing myself so tight against him that bone crunched bone. He gasped, and I swallowed it with a kiss that perversely calmed me, despite the inferno building in my gut.

I broke away. "We need to stop having fuck-hot sex if we're just going to be friends."

Kim's only answer was a groan, coupled with a brutal upward thrust of his hips.

I took the hint and braced myself on the wall, riding him harder until Kim took over, drawing his knees up and driving so deep into me that I saw stars.

Gritting out a curse, I dropped my head to his chest, absorbing the clean scent of his sweat. With him fucking me like this—so rough and raw—I was going to come without touching my dick, a phenomenon that had always blown my mind, but with Kim? Damn. Every nerve in my body was set to explode, and digging my teeth into his tender flesh was the only thing tying me down to the world.

Kim came with a yell, and I followed a heartbeat later, throwing my head back, my mouth open in a silent shout. He shuddered and jerked beneath me, and I shot all over his belly, coming with more force than I could ever remember coming before.

"*Fuck.*" I fell sideways, pulling off Kim's dick a little fast for comfort.

"Easy." Kim rubbed my back. "I've got you."

Oh how I wished that were true, but as breath returned to my lungs, perspective came with it. Jumping on Kim, however willing he might have been, hadn't changed the fact that, in this damn fucking flat, Rich was all I could see.

Perhaps sensing the conflicting chaos brewing in my treacherous brain, Kim shifted and tightened his arms around me. "Don't freak," he said gently. "We're friends, remember? I've *got* you."

The warmth of his embrace was stronger than the simmering heat of our third scorching encounter, but the disquiet in my gut remained. Fucking Kim felt as natural as breathing, but that meant nothing in the cooling light of reality. His lingering relationship with Red bothered me less than I'd assumed it would—if it bothered me at all—but as I pulled back from him and briefly saw nothing in him but Rich's betrayal, I knew that I had a long way to go before I could think of letting this happen between us again.

We dressed in silence.

Perceptive as ever, Kim seemed to know that I didn't want to talk. He pulled his clothes on and drifted back to the window, his lean shoulders framed this time with shadows as the sun disappeared behind the building opposite. "You can't hate him forever, you know. It ain't good for the soul."

"I don't hate Rich." It sounded hollow even to my own ears. "I hate what he *did*. And how it makes—made—me feel."

"Same thing."

Kim didn't turn around. I yanked my T-shirt over my head and went to him, sliding my arms around his waist from behind. "It's not the same thing. I don't think about him anymore. It's just being here . . . it feels like the scene of the crime."

"That why you wanted to fuck me here? Some weird sexual exorcism?"

"Maybe." I couldn't lie to him. "But I would've wanted to fuck you wherever we were."

Kim finally looked at me. I half expected him to be frowning, but his grin was as easy as always. "That's sweet, but we should probably stop fucking each other. No offence, mate, but you seem like you really do need a friend."

That, I couldn't deny. I gave in to the craving to press my face against his back. "You're right . . . about all of it. I guess Red walking in on us did us a favour. Put the brakes on before things got too complicated."

"Things are only as complicated as you allow them to be. I'm not saying we shouldn't *ever* fuck again. Just that you've obviously got some heavy shit weighing you down. And I don't reckon you've done much talking about it, eh?"

I shrugged. "Nope. My family is an open book, but I'm the anomaly. A reticent loner, like my mum."

"You don't have to be alone, Jas. Maybe here"—Kim gestured out of the window—"but not back home. There's a soul for everyone in Porth Ewan, even if it's just a pal to make you a brew when you've been up all night with the moon."

I'd heard it said before that everyone found a friend in Porth Ewan, but as a child I'd never believed it. Running riot on the farm with my brothers every summer, I hadn't needed friends, hadn't wanted them. But *Christ*, I wanted to be Kim's friend. "How are you going to make me a cuppa in the morning if we don't have sleepovers?"

Kim stepped out of my loose hold and turned to face me. "All in good time. Speaking of which, it's getting kinda late. What time does the estate agent's place shut?"

Shit. I glanced at my watch. It was long gone seven, and even with the estate agent's Thursday late-opening hours, getting there before they closed looked like a distant dream.

Damn it. *Always a fucking shambles.* "I gotta go."

I made for the door. Kim got there first. "*We've* gotta go. Friends, remember?"

Well, okay then. There wasn't time to debate his generous interpretation of being my friend. We dashed through Hoxton to the estate agents and made it with seconds to spare. And perhaps because the process was rushed, I didn't feel much as I signed the flat away and handed over the keys.

Or maybe it was Kim's steady presence at my side. His silence was like a blanket wrapped around my shoulders, and later, as we tubed it back to Paddington, I found myself staring at him and trying to imagine the chaos his life must've been when he'd been drinking.

"You thinking about us fucking on your bedroom floor?"

"Huh?" Heat flooded me, as instant as my attraction to him had been when we met. "No, actually, I was thinking about you in a totally different context."

"How so?"

I shrugged. "I'm trying to picture you as a raging alcoholic."

"Why?"

"Because I can't."

"Suits me. Hopefully, you never will."

"Think you'll make it this time?"

It was Kim's turn to shrug. "I try not to think about it at all. Just take each day as it comes."

"Are you tempted a lot?"

"Not on days like this, when I'm distracted by shit that matters. It's harder when I'm bored . . . and alone, which is probably why Lena finds it so hard to stay away, even though she left town six months ago."

I could imagine other reasons why Red would find it difficult to stay away from Kim, but I kept those to myself. If Kim didn't know how much I wanted him by now, then we'd been screwing each other all wrong. "I like being alone. Need it sometimes—the peace and quiet, the solitude. I can't think straight when I spend too much time with other people."

"Ah, so that's why you never thought it was weird that your ex was away so much? Because it suited you not to?"

"I guess so."

The tube wobbled into Paddington and jolted to a stop, throwing us against each other. The contact was electric, and my breath caught in my chest, but the doors opened before I could cross the invisible line we'd sketched in the sand since we'd left my Hoxton flat behind.

We got off the train and rode the escalators up into the overground station, Kim still guarding the photos and his precious wood. In the main ticket hall, we found the big screens awash with red, all the trains heading south-west cancelled.

Shit. I scanned the screens, searching for a way home, more eager to escape London than I'd ever been, but the situation—whatever it was—seemed to get worse by the second.

Kim touched my arm. "There's a sleeper heading out from platform nine. We'll have to leg it, though. It leaves in two minutes."

How he'd seen that in the mess of red on the screens, I had no idea, but I took his word for it and set off at a run, following the bustle of people who'd obviously had the same idea. The sleeper trains took all night to reach Truro, but a seven-hour train ride was better than no train at all.

At least, I thought so, until I remembered too late that sleeper trains were mainly made up of two-man cabins. And as luck would have it—or not—the only spaces left on the train was a single seat next to the communal toilet, or a cabin with the world's smallest double cot.

"Take the cabin," the Network Rail worker said. "Your

tickets aren't usually valid for the Night Riviera, so make the most of it. Got phone chargers and everything."

Like I gave a fuck about charging my phone, which was just as well as it turned out the phone "charger" was a two-pin AC plug socket.

Kim dropped his bag by the tiny bed. "You can have it, if you like. I can sit in the seat."

As if. I stuck my head out of the cabin door. "Neither of us can sit in the seat. It's taken."

"Oh."

Oh, indeed. I sat gingerly on the bed and wondered what Kim was thinking. Was the idea of sharing an actual bed with me so horrible? Or was he doubting that we'd make it all the way home without fucking again?

His face gave nothing away as he sat down beside me, but his jaw-cracking yawn implied the latter was unlikely. I leaned into him, closing my eyes briefly as he did the same. "Thank you for coming with me. I'd probably be in some arse-end pub by now if you hadn't, or some dodgy gay bar. I tend to put my dick in all the wrong places when I'm upset."

"So much for solitude."

"Solitude is my sober happy space. Drunk me is needy as fuck."

"Nice."

"Not really." I didn't have to look at Kim to know he agreed, but I did anyway and found nothing but acceptance in his steady gaze. Part of me yearned for a reaction, for judgement, but most of me was eternally grateful that he saw the worst of me and didn't seem to mind it. "Sex addiction is a thing, right?"

He nodded. "I've met a few sex addicts in rehab, and it's supposed to be one of the toughest addictions to beat."

"No magic pill, eh?"

"There's no magic pill for anything." Kim lay back and closed his eyes, his body rocking with the motion of the train as it pulled out of Paddington. "You just have to find better ways of coping with reality."

Reality. Huh. For me, that meant a long journey home to a new flat that was, by design, even more lonely than my life in Hoxton had become. Or did it? Perhaps it didn't need to be that way. I kept my family at arm's length by choice, and rarely saw them outside of the farm, but Kim and I had vowed to be friends, real friends, and I couldn't imagine feeling alone with him by my side.

I looked down at him. Lying back with his feet still on the floor, he couldn't be comfortable. I nudged him, absorbing his sleepy groan like a warmth-starved vulture. "Get in the bed. There's a duvet and everything. We can top and tail, if you like?"

"Top and tail?" Kim cracked an eye open. "After we've both been hoofing around London all day? Fuck that."

"Fair enough. You take the duvet, I'll sleep on top."

Kim sighed and pulled the duvet back. "Jesus, Jas, just get in. I'm sure we can manage a few hours kip without ruining our beautiful friendship."

Put like that, how could I argue? Besides, as Kim rolled onto the bed, there was no way I could resist the call to slide in behind him, moulding my body to the curve of his, all the while leaving as much distance between us as the narrow bed allowed.

Kim chuckled.

In the dim light of the room I imagined his knowing grin lighting up his face. "What are you laughing at?"

"Would you still be my friend if I said I was laughing at you?"

"Probably."

"Would you still be my friend if I asked you to put your arms around me?"

I sat up, propping myself on my elbow, and peered over his shoulder. His eyes were closed, but the set of his jaw was different somehow, like vulnerability had crept into him while I hadn't been looking. I put my hands on him and scooted closer. It was on the tip of my tongue to tell him I'd wrap my arms around him anytime he wanted, but I said nothing as I pulled him close and buried my face against his neck.

Didn't need to.

Hundreds of miles from home, rocking in limbo on a train that smelled of damp and stale sausage rolls, I only needed him.

I didn't see Kim for a week or so after our random London trip. He drove me home from Truro station in a van that stank of chicken shit, and then disappeared into the gloomy early morning, leaving me to immerse myself in a design job that was a world away from the rustic barn back on the farm.

Pharmaceutical companies. Ugh. I'd branded one as a favour to an old friend a few years ago, and somehow it had become a thing—too sterile to keep me inspired, but too lucrative to ignore. A fact I found truly depressing as the days slipped by in a dull haze of bland corporate logos.

A week into the project found me half-mad with boredom. One night, in a fit of rebellion, I shut down my technical drawing software and opened the folder of photos from Red's band gig—the hot and heady rock concert that had brought Kim and me together with a literal bang. There was no reason for me to fiddle with the images—the good ones had long ago been sent to the band's manager and plastered all over their socials—but something drew me to my favourite shot of Red.

I opened the image, splashing her all over my twenty-seven-inch iMac screen. Dressed all in black, her hair a riot against her pale, inked skin, she was as stunning now as she'd been that night. But it wasn't just her I saw as I zoomed in on her curves, rotating the image this way and that. Kim had been on my mind since the day I met him, but the pang in my chest as I thought of him now was new, and I realised with a start that I missed him, even though I had no bloody right to.

With a head full of slender bones and tattoos, I went to bed, for once sleeping through the night and waking up at a respectable time. My dreams had been filled with the gentle motion of the sleeper train, and I woke half expecting to find Kim in my arms, like I had that hazy morning when the train had passed through Taunton.

I didn't, obviously, and the disappointment of finding myself alone was harsh enough to drive me from my bed and out of my minimalist flat. The seafront was moody and damp, my favourite kind of morning, despite the perpetual grey tones that took a bit of processing to bring my shots to life.

Camera in hand, I roamed the promenade, snapping anything that took my fancy—the people, the seagulls, the frothy waves. A steady trickle of youngish folk disappearing down one of the cobbled side streets caught my eye. It took me a while to figure out that they must've been heading to one of Porth Ewan's biggest off-peak attractions: Blood Rush, the tattoo studio Kim worked for.

Curiosity was an evil thing. It would've been so easy to just go home, but of course, I didn't. Instead, I shouldered my camera and followed a girl with tangerine-coloured hair all the way to the door of the gothic-punk studio.

Distracted by the vintage photographs in the window, I didn't go in.

I was still studying them when I sensed a presence beside me—a slim, inked-up presence that definitely *wasn't* Kim. In fact, I was fairly certain that I was staring into the keen eyes of Brix Lusmoore.

A theory confirmed as the man extended his hand. "Brix," he said. "You're Gaz's brother, ain't ya? Jasper?"

I shook Brix's hand. "Jas, but you're right about the rest, and we've met before, actually, when you brought my old man some chickens. Where did you get these images? They're awesome."

"Me and Kim rescued them from my fella's old flat in London. He'd forgotten he had them."

"You got lucky. That's Pam Nash, isn't it?"

"Think so. We've got some Les Skuse in the back too. Want to see?"

More than he knew, but the thought of barging, uninvited, into yet another part of Kim's life felt wrong.

With teeth gnashing regret, I shook my head.

Brix grinned, wry and wise, and looked as though he would disappear back inside the studio, but his path was suddenly blocked.

Red. She smiled. "You've kept me waiting."

"That so? Didn't know you were expecting me."

"Then you don't know much at all." She put her hands on her hips. "Did you think I'd let you take such fantastic pictures of me without saying thank you?"

It hadn't occurred to me that she'd want to thank me—at least, not in person. The band's manager had paid my invoice ten minutes after I'd sent it, and I'd considered the transaction complete. "You don't need to thank me. You and the band made my job easy."

The band. Right. I'd taken hundreds of images that night, but only Red's stuck in my mind, and I got the feeling that she knew it as her smile morphed into something close to a smirk.

"Come inside," she said. "Unless you fancy a coffee next door?"

I said goodbye to an amused Brix, and chose the coffee.

"So . . ." Red said when she'd hustled me to a table at the back of the café next door to the studio. "I think I owe you an apology."

I stirred way too much sugar into my espresso. "How'd you work that out?"

"I walked in on you and Kim like I owned the place, and I shouldn't have."

"So, why did you?" Kim had already explained it in far more detail than I was entitled to, but for some reason, I needed to hear it from her.

Red shrugged. "He was mine to walk in on whenever I liked for so long, I sometimes forget that he's not anymore. And it's not often that he has reason to care whether I walk in or not."

"Because you join in? Shit, sorry. That was rude."

"Not at all, but you're wrong, as it goes. Me and Kim...we had an open relationship that worked for both of us, but we haven't been together for a while now—not even to play."

I took a slow, scalding sip of my over-sweetened coffee. "He's told me a little bit about that, but it's not really any of my business."

"Unless you want it to be."

It wasn't a question, but I turned it over in my mind as I watched Red's throat work as she swallowed a sip of herbal tea. "I'm not sure either of us is ready for anything more than we've already had. We're friends . . . kind of."

"Kim has enough friends."

"So? There's no room for a little one?"

Red put her elbows on the table. "Okay, real talk now. You know what I'm trying to say, even though Kim would bloody *kill* me if he knew I was sticking my oar in like this. Look, Jas, *please* . . . don't judge Kim by something you don't understand. He deserves better than that. I'd imagine you both do."

"I haven't judged him." But as the words left my mouth, I remembered that they weren't true, because I *had* judged Kim, and her, from the moment I'd realised that their sexual relationship might not be entirely over.

Like she'd read my mind—seen through my unintentional lie—she leaned forward. "We're not slutty, *Jasper*. It's just a different way of living."

The way she said my name did odd things to the jacked-up coffee in my stomach. For a brief and bizarre moment, I wanted to grip her chin and implore *her* to listen to *me*, but I said nothing. Just stared, like the idiot I was, until I found my tongue. "Kim and I are friends, and I don't judge him for anything. I admire him, actually. He's like no one I've ever known."

"Then you should probably tell him that. His opinion of himself sometimes needs a little bolstering."

"And you can't do that?"

"Don't make me kick you under this table, because I bloody will."

I didn't doubt it for a second as I raised my hands in surrender. "When I see him next, I'll tell him, I promise."

Not that I had any idea when that would be. I'd thought about calling Kim a thousand times, but I hadn't. And he hadn't called me. Perhaps it was a sign to let sleeping dogs lie—

Red kicked me sharply in the shin with her purple Doc Martens. "Don't be a dick. Kim's my best friend and I won't give him up for anyone, but he's never looked at me the way I've seen him looking at you. Don't waste that, because you have no idea how lucky you are."

The rumble of a motorbike drowned out any reply I may have made. The same Harley I'd seen at Kim's place pulled up and Red tipped me a final glare before she pushed her chair back and left.

She climbed onto the back of the Harley, and I noticed it was flanked by three others. Three *men*. With their helmets and riding leathers, I couldn't tell if it was the same group I'd nearly photographed at the jam festival, but either way, I heeded the first words Kim had ever spoken to me and kept my curiosity to myself as they roared away with Red.

That left me alone with my empty coffee cup. I scraped at a few stubborn grains of sugar with a teaspoon, willing the burn in my chest to fade. It had been a long time since a woman had ripped me a new one over a cup of coffee. And what to do about it? My encounter with Red hadn't changed the fact that I was still too busy sulking about Rich to give Kim the attention he deserved. Which meant whatever Red thought, *Kim* was right: we were better as friends.

After downing another brutal shot of coffee, I tramped back home and got on with the pharmaceutical project. By the evening, it was done. I uploaded the files and shut up shop for the night. I fancied a pint, but logic told me that the pub was the last place I'd find Kim, so I got in my car and drove out to the commune.

And as luck would have it, Kim was at the end of the path, loading up the bumper-sized recycling bin. I pulled up and wound down the passenger window. "Searching for scraps?"

"Chucking them out, more like." Kim let the bin lid drop and hopped down onto the grass verge. "What brings you out here?"

"Looking for you. Didn't think I'd find you in the Sea Bell."

"You'd be surprised, actually. I spend as much time in there as I do my ma's house."

"It's not triggering for you?"

Kim shrugged. "Nah, being home alone triggers me."

"Home alone now?"

"Yup."

I leaned over and opened the door. "Get in."

Life was never simple. Kim had a flock of chickens to round up before he could go anywhere, a task that was, after many summers at Belly Acre, familiar. I helped guide a couple of dozen birds into hen houses that wouldn't have been out of place in Camden Town. "Damn. You made these?"

"Apparently. I was off the wagon at the time."

Looking more closely at the paintwork on the nearest wooden structure, it showed. The chaotic colour held none of the calm beauty of Kim's usual pieces. "Still pretty good, though. Every cloud, eh?"

Kim rolled his eyes and bolted the doors on both hen houses. "If you say so. I only kept them because they were gonna get covered in shit anyway."

Fair enough. I nudged him. "Ready?"

"Hmm? Oh, yeah . . . sure. Where are we going?"

I had no idea, but it didn't seem to matter as we got in my car and hit the road, chasing the fading sun as it sank into the horizon. If I'd been alone, I'd have followed it to the beach and shot a lonely long exposure, but I hadn't sought Kim out to ditch him for my camera, so I drove instead to the highest point in Porth Ewan and parked up at the cliff edge.

Kim took his seat belt off and tipped his seat back. "How did you know?"

"Know what?"

"That this is my favourite place to be when I feel like this?"

"I don't know how you feel."

"No?" Kim closed his eyes. "Coulda fooled me."

I let him be for a while, entertained enough by the sunset that was fast becoming a stormy night sky. My hand found its way to Kim's leg and lay there, passive and available.

Inevitable.

I had no idea how much time had passed when he finally took it and laced our fingers together. He didn't speak, and I didn't care. Quiet was my thing. I enjoyed it, I craved it, and a Porth Ewan silence was a special thing indeed.

We were in total darkness by the time Kim let out a soft sigh. "Lena came to see me earlier. Said she shouted at you in Becky's."

It took me a moment to pair my encounter with Red to the name of the coffee shop beside Blood Rush. "There wasn't much shouting. She did boot me one, though."

"Shit. Sorry. She's got a bee in her bonnet about me being a terminal bachelor."

The theory didn't quite match with the free-loving lifestyle I'd come to associate with Kim and Red. I said as much, and Kim chuckled darkly. "All the fuck-hot sex in the world doesn't stop you being lonely."

"I'd settle for the fuck-hot sex."

"I don't give you that?"

More silence. I wondered if Kim might zone out again, but he didn't. He squeezed my hand and fixed me with a gaze that made the tempestuous night brewing outside fade to nothing. "I kept fucking Lena for a while after we split because she's my safe place, whether either of us are seeing other people or not. Being with you is different."

"Different?"

"Yeah. I don't fuck you because I want to . . .it's because I *need* to, and I don't know how I'm going to give that up."

"So don't. We both need a friend and we both need to fuck, right?"

I said it with a grin, but the humour was loaded, and Kim looked away. "You do realise we spend way too much time talking about this, don't you?"

"Not especially, but I'm hoping we'll figure it out soon."

"Me too. You're on my mind a lot, which is probably why Lena came after you. She worries about me when I'm quiet."

"She didn't come after me."

"No?" Kim treated me to another intense stare. "What the fuck happened, then? I didn't exactly give her a chance to explain."

"I was talking to Brix outside the studio. She came out, and we went next door for a coffee. I'm sure she's told you the rest."

"Only that she was a dick."

"She wasn't a dick."

"Her words, not mine." Kim smiled tiredly. "Argue the toss with her."

"No, thanks. I'm still bruised from losing the last round." I rubbed my thumb over Kim's tattooed knuckles. "For what it's worth, though, I think she just wants you to be happy."

Kim sighed. "Oh, I know that. I guess I'm a bit depressed. It happens now and then, especially when something good happens in my life. Weird, eh?"

Being mildly miserable had become my baseline, so I had to take his word for it. Besides, speculating about the new positivity in his life was distracting. "Would it help if we fucked on the car bonnet?"

"Probably. Bit cold for alfresco nookie, though."

He had me there. "Listen—"

"Look—" he said at the same time, turning to face me.

"Go on," I said.

He shrugged. "It's stupid when I say it out loud."

"Not as stupid as what I was about to say."

"You should go first, then."

It was on the tip of my tongue to refuse, but the sad fire in Kim's eyes had faded a touch, perhaps lightened by my awkward attempts at humour, and the reckless numbnut in me figured I had nothing to lose. "This friends thing we've got going on. Any chance we could add in some, uh—"

"Benefits?"

I tightened my grip on his hand. "For lack of a better word, yeah. I mean, everything we said before still stands, but it feels kinda wrong to ignore . . . whatever this is completely."

"Sounds like the kind of shit we could talk about for another week."

"Or not. I haven't seen you since we went to the city."

Kim sighed again. "That's because you fucking scare me."

"Me? How?"

"By looking at me and seeing the bloke I was meant to be before I ballsed it all up. I forget, sometimes, when I'm with you, that the rest of it ever happened."

I couldn't begin to understand the weight behind his words. Instead I turned in my seat and gripped his chin with my spare hand in much the same way I'd imagined myself gripping Red's earlier. "Then be with me . . . as my friend."

"A friend with benefits? Cos that's all my junkyard heart is good for these days."

The reference to the commune made me smile, but the sentiment made me want to weep. I hooked my hand behind his neck and pulled him close, knowing that I had to speak before we kissed, because the moment our lips met, my mind would be devoid of all else, of all reason, of anything except the way Kim felt in my arms.

I sucked in a shaky breath and dragged my thumb over his cheekbone. "Your heart isn't junk to me."

CHAPTER
NINE

You'd think that after spending all evening talking about it, we'd have spent the rest of the night fucking. We didn't. After a kiss that went on far longer than any in my adult life, I drove Kim home and left him at the end of the path that led to the commune.

And tried not to wonder if there'd be a light on in his trailer when he walked into the orchard, because as much as I wanted to deny it, I was still too intrigued by the idea of Kim and Red together—her curves against his slender bones. With me, he was a dominant lover. Was he the same with her? Or did he lie at her mercy? And why did it even matter? Kim was Kim, and if we had any chance of making our own brand of friendship work, I had to accept that. I *wanted* to accept it, and I did.

I *was* curious, though, which outweighed my brief period of jealousy. And I wanted to know Red better, know the woman Kim struggled to give up. All I had to do was find a way to spend time with her without getting booted in the shin.

A few days after Kim and I had been to the cliffs, I met him at Belly Acre Farm. He'd come to see the progress in the barn, and I'd pretty much ditched everything to be there to show him around, a turn of events that amused my brothers to no end.

"You're blatantly shagging him," Gaz said. "Can't think of another reason you'd be mooning around at the gatepost."

I gave him the finger, unwilling to admit that he'd caught me loitering at the top of the driveway doing just that. "Perhaps *he's* blatantly shagging *me*."

Predictably, Gaz cringed and wandered off. Davey, a few years younger and far less freaked out by man sex, wasn't as easily dismissed. "Is he doing the doors as well as the furniture?"

"No idea. Ask Dad."

Davey leaned on the fence beside me. "You know he's got a girlfriend, right?"

"Dad has? Damn, that mean you've got another illegitimate sibling on the way?"

"Don't be a dick."

"Don't *you* be a dick. If you're talking about Kim, don't bother. I know about him and Red."

"Who the fuck's Red? I'm talking about Lena Gordon. Her and Kim have been together for years, everyone knows."

I snorted. "Everyone knows? Since when did everyone know anything about anyone? Grow the fuck up."

"Suit yourself." Davey pushed himself off the fence as a vehicle engine rumbled at the end of the driveway. "Just saying what I heard."

He walked away, leaving me to feel bad for being a prick. I hadn't had many relationships, but every bisexual I'd ever known had suffered through the same thing—the insistence that you had to choose one way or the other, that you couldn't commit to another soul without drawing a line under your sexuality, *and* that all men who claimed to swing both ways were living the same life as Rich.

Briefly, I felt bad for Rich too, that he was so fucked up he had to live a lie to survive, but that shit didn't last long. I was learning to curb the negativity that came with any thought of Rich, but he wasn't getting my sympathy. Fuck no.

A Ford KA pulled up in front of me. I couldn't contain my amusement as Kim practically fell out the driver door. "I don't think I've seen you drive the same car twice. Don't tell me this is yours?"

Kim laughed, regaining his trademark grace as he straightened up. "It's Lena's. She leaves it with me when she leaves, and I like driving it."

"Because it's pink?"

"Yup. And it's a good reminder to check myself. A mate sprayed it for her to punish me for tipping her black Golf into a ditch when I was wankered."

"When was this?"

"A long time ago. I only got my licence back last month."

Sometimes I chose to forget the destruction Kim's addiction must have wreaked on those around him. I waited until he got close enough and then pulled him in for a quick hug, brushing his cheek with a kiss. "It suits you. The pink, I mean. Not many blokes could own it."

"I know a few who could. You're one of them."

"Thanks."

Kim shrugged. "You're the coolest motherfucker I've ever known."

He thinks I'm cool? As hard as I tried, I couldn't quite believe it. I was a nerd—tied to my computer when I wasn't surgically attached to my camera—and no match for the mellow poise that rolled off Kim. "So . . . you wanna see the barn?"

"Lead on."

I took Kim to the barn, which, minus the furniture and some new doors, was well on its way to being finished. The kitchen was up and running too.

Kim sniffed the air. "Pasties?"

"You Porth Ewan boys can smell them a mile off, eh?"

Kim's grin concurred. I rolled my eyes and meandered to the kitchen to swipe him one from the plate Laura was bound to have left out for thieving fingers.

I came back with a plain pasty and one of the spicy variations. Kim swiped the spicy one. Thank fuck. As much as I loved Gaz's ginger-mango chutney, I couldn't handle too much heat.

Kim laughed. "I thought emmets liked fucking with tradition? Calum loves this shit."

Emmet. It had been a while since I'd last been called that. And I was Cornish enough to ride Kim's dick, so he could jog on with that bullshit.

I gave him the finger and turned away, drifting towards the area of the barn that had been designated as the canteen. "The rest of your tables and chairs will go here."

Kim scanned the area, slowing the short work he'd made of his pasty. "And I've got three weeks to finish them?"

"If you say so." I'd been caught up enough in my own deadlines that the barn's schedule had slipped my mind. "Are you on track?"

"As much as I ever am with anything."

Kim's tone spun me around to face him properly. He was brushing crumbs from his hands—eyes down, head bowed—and his expression was hard to gauge, but something was off.

I came back to him and nudged his arm. "Everything okay?"

"Hmm?" Kim jumped, startled by my touch. "Sorry, what?"

"Checking you're okay. Got a weight on your mind?"

He offered me a weak half smile that did nothing to ease my concern. "No more than usual. Ignore me, mate. Probably hungry."

"You just ate."

"Be right as rain soon enough, then, eh?"

I wasn't convinced. Perhaps I'd been spoiled by his easy disposition. Still, there wasn't much I could do if he wasn't prepared to tell me. Maybe a distraction would help. "Do you want to see my dad's veg field? The lettuces are done, but the raspberries and pumpkins are looking good. There's tomatoes in the poly-tunnels too."

Genuine enthusiasm brightened Kim's face, so endearing it hurt, and I couldn't resist taking his hand as we left the barn and walked through the yard towards the fields.

He didn't object, and the way he laced his fingers with mine took me back to our cliff-top evening a few days ago, reminding me that I *had* seen him off his game before. He'd vaguely blamed drink-demons then. Was that the problem now?

It felt weird to ask. So I didn't. I took him to my dad's fruit and veg fields and tried not to jump him while he examined each and every plant and asked me a million questions about soil and seasonal watering.

Questions I had *no idea* how to answer. Which was, apparently, enough to cheer him up. "How can you live here and not have a clue how anything works?"

"I don't live here."

"Yeah, but you were raised here . . . kinda. How can you be so detached?"

Detached. The playful accusation stung, though I couldn't say why. "I know where the kitchen is, if you fancy a cuppa. That do you?"

The humour in Kim's beautiful face faded. "Actually, I should be getting back. I've left the lads sanding the tabletops so I can paint them tonight."

"Sure? There's plum cake?"

Kim growled low in his throat. "You're a fucker, you know that?"

"What?"

Kim shook his head. "Never mind."

"Fuck, no. Don't pull that shit on me. If I've pissed you off, tell me. I can't fix it otherwise."

"Do you want to fix it?"

"What's that supposed to mean?"

Kim stood from where he'd been studying the soil around my dad's biggest pumpkin. "What are we doing, Jas? Every time I think I know, five minutes with you confuses the fuck out of me."

"I thought we were friends?"

"Friends that fuck, but we don't do a whole lot of that either."

"You're pissed off because we don't fuck enough?"

If Kim was confused, I was nothing short of bewildered. Our friendship was complicated, but it had seemed like we'd made progress in recent days.

Kim sighed. "I . . . Fuck, I don't know. I think I'm just tired. I don't sleep much when I'm on my own."

"Red not with you?"

"*No.* She has her own trailer in the fucking woods. I thought you knew that?"

Did I? Neither one of them had given me the impression

that Red lived with Kim, but I'd kind of assumed that Kim was never alone.

Dickhead. Alone the other night, wasn't he?

And, twat that I was, I couldn't seem to help sticking my foot in it further. "My brother told me that you and Red are still together."

"Your brother? Which one?"

"Davey."

"Never met the bloke. What the fuck does he know about my life?"

"Nothing. Just putting it out there that it's not only me who's sending mixed messages."

Anger flashed in Kim's suddenly piercing gaze. "What mixed messages? I was honest about Lena, and I haven't been with her since I met you. What more do you want from me?"

"Been with her? As in—"

"As in shagged her, Jas. Cos that's all you're bothered about, right? Who screws who? Not that she's my best friend in the world? Not that it's really fucking hard to let go of the one person who's always had my back? Who's forgiven me for every fuckup I've had?"

The fury in his rant caught me off guard. "I've never asked you to give her up."

"Why not?"

He had me there. Even if he had slept with Red in the time since we'd met, he hadn't cheated on me, because I'd given him nothing to be unfaithful to. "Because I don't want you to give her up."

"Because you don't want me?"

"No, because I don't—I *can't*—feel threatened by something that means so much."

"Fuck this." Kim dodged me as I reached for him. "Look,

just forget it, okay? It is what it is between us—some shit-hot sex and mates, yeah? Shame we can't have a pint together. We'd be laughing then."

"Kim—"

"No. I gotta go. I've got loads to do tonight, and I reckon you've seen enough of me for one day."

That would never happen, but instead of saying so, my tongue stuck to the roof of my mouth, and Kim was halfway to Red's ridiculous pink car before I took a step forward.

And by then it was too late. Kim was out of earshot and, it seemed, out of the flawed brand of friendship I'd kidded myself that I could handle.

Kim didn't call. And I didn't call him, which meant we were back in the silent phase of our never-ending cycle of bullshit and miscommunication.

I blamed myself. How could I not? Everything Kim had said to me was true. I'd asked to be friends, and then screwed him on the floor of my old flat. Then I'd asked him to be a friend I could fuck, only to drive him home with no more than a snog on the doorstep, all the while giving him no indication that I gave a shit what became of us.

The Red thing wasn't quite as he saw it, though, but it would take a hell of a conversation for him to believe that. Despite what Rich had put me through, I truly had no problem with the bond Kim and Red had forged long before I knew them. How could I, when he'd been so honest about it?

Besides, it wasn't Rich's *wife* who'd hurt me so much, it had been the lies, the deception . . . the hidden side of a man I'd believed I would spend the rest of my life with. I didn't know Kim as well as I wanted to, and I didn't know Red at all, but somehow I believed *in* them, a notion that made little sense as I threw myself into my work in an effort to give Kim some space.

Space. Ha. Would I never fucking learn? When a week of silence turned into ten long days, it appeared not. Tail between my legs, I got in my car one Saturday afternoon and drove to the commune, but there was no one there, and no sign of Red's pink car.

Deflated, I wound up at the farm, seeking shelter in Laura's kitchen while the others were all out painting the barn to match the new doors Kim had apparently delivered the day before.

"We didn't expect him to have them finished so soon." Laura set her gigantic teapot on the table. "He surprised us when he turned up last night."

"Was he okay?"

Laura arched an eyebrow. "Okay? Yes, he seemed to be, not that he said much. We couldn't even tempt him in with a glass of your dad's blackberry wine."

"He doesn't drink, ma. He's an alcoholic."

"Oh." For once, my wonderful stepmother appeared lost for words. "Well, he doesn't look like one."

I rolled my eyes. "Who does?"

"Is he a functioning alcoholic? I've read about those."

"*Ma*, I have no idea what you read about in those daft magazines of yours."

"Cheeky." Laura cuffed my ear as she claimed the seat beside me, softening the blow with a plate of jam-filled shortbread. "But I'm sorry if I've put my foot in my mouth. Us old fogies have to work hard to keep up."

"You're not that old."

"Old enough to know better than to talk when I should be listening."

Knowing that resistance was futile, I took my cue. "I think I've fucked up."

"How?"

I reached for a biscuit and set about crumbling it into sticky dust. "Me and Kim . . . we, um—"

"Hooked up? I read about that too, in *Heat*."

"Hope you lit it on fire afterwards. But, yeah, if we're being millennial about it, we met at that hippie fest a while back, and then at a gig in Porth Luck. We hooked up and things have been, uh, complicated ever since."

Laura poured tea. "Because of his drinking?"

"He doesn't drink, I told you. And it's me, not him."

"Ah." Laura stirred milk slowly into a rose-adorned mug that was older than me. "Does this have anything to do with what happened with Rich?"

I cast her a sideways glance. I'd never gone into detail with my family about why Rich and I had split, but I wasn't naïve enough to believe I'd hidden the resulting carnage from them. "Kind of. After Rich, I didn't think I was ready for more than sex, and I liked Kim too much to just have that with him, so we agreed to be friends."

"Friends is nice," Laura said. "What went wrong?"

"Everything." I dumped my elbows on the table. "For one, we kept having sex, and then there's Red to consider."

"Red?"

"His missus, well . . . ex-missus, but they're still—"

"Hooking up?"

"Close." I searched for the words to explain it to my sweet step-mother. "They love each other, and that's not going to change."

"I see. Is that a bad thing?"

And that, right there, was why I'd come to Laura. Her unconditional love for my father was the reason my childhood

had been so full and bright, instead of broken by the resent-
ment of a woman who'd never asked for an extra child, or the
dull monotony of my actual mother's irritation that I existed at
all. "No, actually, and whether he fucks her or not doesn't
make a huge amount of difference to me."

Laura sipped at her tea. "Would you like to sleep with her
too?"

"I don't think so." And of that I was almost certain. I'd
been sexually attracted to women in the past, and Red was
stunning, but my fascination with her was all about Kim. "I
don't know her, to be honest."

"But you like her?"

"Platonically," I admitted, because it was true. My encoun-
ters with Red had endeared me to her, even if she had left a
vicious bruise on my shin. How could it not, when it was clear
her frustration had stemmed from a primal instinct to protect
Kim? "I just don't know where we go from here, though. I'm a
disaster, ma. What if I screw his life up? Mess with his recovery? Or him and Red?"

"What makes you think your presence in his life will be
negative? What happened with Rich wasn't your fault."

"Wasn't it?"

"No, it bloody wasn't."

I blinked. Laura rarely swore, even in a house full of blokes
who cursed like sailors. "Why are you so sure?"

"Because, Jasper, I raised you every summer your mother
saw fit to let me, and I know you only show your affection
when you truly mean it. You loved that man, and he hurt you.
That *wasn't* your fault. My concern now is that you've taken it
to mean that's all you're good for."

". . . *my junkyard heart*."

"I don't think that."

"No? Then what's keeping you and Kim apart?"

I shrugged. "Everything. Nothing. I don't know if he wants to be with me, I just know that what we have at the moment is hurting him."

"Because it's making him feel like he's not good enough."

It wasn't a question, and she was on the money. I put my head in my hands. "God, I fucking hate myself for making him feel that way."

"There'll be more to it, if he's struggling with other things."

"He probably wouldn't tell me if he was. He's so easygoing, but he doesn't talk . . . he's like, I don't know, a perfect contradiction."

Laura smiled. "All the best men are, dear. They'd be boring if you always knew what they were thinking."

"What should I do?"

"Whatever feels right, and no one knows that but you."

If only it were that easy. I drank the rest of my tea, only half listening to Laura talk about how her unconventional relationship with my father had made Belly Acre Farm the gossip of Porth Ewan when I'd been born. I envied her, I truly did. She'd always been so sure of her path, so sure that her soul told her the truth—that no matter what, or who, crossed into her life, my father's heart was hers.

On cue, my dad came in from the barn, paint splattered all over him, a crate of potatoes in his arms. "Okay, son?"

I nodded. I loved him, but I couldn't talk to him like I could Laura, and he respected that, trusting that I'd come to him if I needed him.

I rarely did.

Still, his hand on my arm as he passed was comforting, though the smell of freshly dug potatoes reminded me that, in a fit of Kim-fuelled madness, I'd agreed to help Davey at the imminent autumn fair.

Great.

Kim's workshop had a stall not far from ours. Whether he wanted to or not, he'd be spending most of that day staring right at me. Could I wait that long?

Logic said I'd have to.

My heart said fuck no.

CHAPTER
TEN

My heart said fuck no . . .

But Laura said yes. "He wasn't home an hour ago, and it won't do you any harm to get a square meal in you before you go charging off."

Stupidly, I let her force me to stay for dinner—a rowdy family meal that was only bearable by numbing my eardrums with a couple of glasses of my dad's homemade wine. I was half-pissed before it occurred to me that my car was the only way I had of getting my sorry arse to the commune.

Shit. I stood in the yard, glaring at the car, the realisation that I was over the limit sinking in, thick and fast. The knob-head in me wanted to blame Laura for making me stay, but she hadn't passed me the wine—Gaz had, and *he* hadn't forced me to drink it.

Nope. That shit was all mine.

Gaz appeared at my side. "I'd drive you home myself, but I've had a skinful. Tell you what: you can borrow my old BMX if you like."

He said it like it was the funniest thing in the world, and drifted back inside, his laughter ringing out in the quiet yard, but the idea had legs. I hadn't ridden a bike in years, but as I dragged the cobweb-covered bicycle out of the shed and poked at the half-flat tyres, it didn't seem to matter. You never forgot, right?

Wrong. Turned out wobble-cycling, fuelled by too much wine, wasn't as much fun as I might've imagined if I'd been sober enough to imagine anything. And Blackbeard's Junkyard was further away than I'd thought. My legs were like fragile new wheat fronds by the time it came into view.

I ditched the bike and scaled the wooden fence. No one seemed to be around, but there was soft acoustic music in the air, and the scent of gently spiced cooking. I followed the path to the orchard, sobering up with every step as the prospect of seeing Kim warmed my bones, and my legs carried me to the door of his trailer of their own volition.

The door was ajar with a haze of heady incense smoke drifting out to greet me. I considered knocking, but something —likely my dad's dodgy wine—gave me some brash courage, and I nudged the door all the way open.

I couldn't say if I'd imagined that I'd find Kim alone, or if I'd expected him to be home at all, because my ride to the commune had passed in a blur of looming ditches and precarious peddling. And the scene I stumbled into didn't shock me or even surprise me. Why would it, when I'd pictured it—or tried to—near enough every day since I'd met Kim?

Red noticed me first, from her position stretched out like a cat on the very rug Kim had fucked me on all those weeks ago. Her smile was softly dazzling, and she poked Kim, rousing him from his apparent fixation with the log burner.

He blinked. "Jas."

"Hey." I took a step forward, then stopped, the fact that Red was dressed only in Kim's T-shirt finally sinking in. "Um . . . sorry, I don't want to interrupt."

"You're not." Red held out her hand, beckoning me closer. "Kim was just showing me all the yummy jams and stuff your family have on their website. I think I'll have to raid their stock before I go home."

"When are you going home?"

I was genuinely curious, but my tone must've suggested otherwise, because Red let her hand drop and gracefully got to her feet, revealing that she was, actually, wearing shorts beneath Kim's T-shirt. "I'll be gone before you know it, sweetheart. I can leave right now, if you like."

"Why would I like that?"

"You tell me, *Jasper*."

Jasper. Goddamn. I'd spent my whole life trying to convince people to overlook my full name, but Red had a way of wrapping her tongue around it that made me forget Kim's ominous silence.

Briefly, because there was no forgetting Kim when he was suddenly in front of me, his gaze as intense as it had ever been. More so. "Are you drunk?"

I winced. "A bit. Sorry, I was halfway here before I figured it might be a problem for you, and by then—" I waved a hand. "I'm sorry."

"Don't be. My problems aren't yours."

"What if I want them to be?"

"Why would you want that?"

"Why not?"

"Dear God." Red laughed. "You've met your evasive match there, Kimmie. No wonder you've been pissing in circles for weeks."

That she seemed to know enough about Kim and me to

make that judgement seemed oddly normal. And it was reassuring to know that Kim's habitual deflection wasn't all about me.

But I didn't look at Red. Couldn't, because I had eyes just for Kim as I took his face in my hands and kissed him, really kissed him, falling into him the way I should've been falling all along.

Falling into his arms.

Falling in love.

Because I could love him, and he could love me, if only we'd both stop sitting down at the foot of the hill.

Kim let out a surprised grunt, but didn't resist as I backed him against the trailer's thin wall. And I didn't stop my assault on his mouth, even when lips that weren't Kim's brushed a soft kiss to the back of my neck.

Red's touch was fleeting, and thrilling. I didn't notice where she went, but I smelled her sweet, feminine scent mingling with the lingering incense smoke, and with Kim's unique essence of wood, paint, and ink.

If I'd been drunk before, I was intoxicated now. I craved Kim's skin against mine, and I fumbled with his T-shirt, yanking it over his head like we were alone. He returned the favour and his chest hit mine. I closed my eyes, wading through the quagmire of complication we'd created between us, chasing the healthy oblivion that was a world away from our shared demons.

The solitude I'd spent years craving was a distant memory as I gently swiped Kim's legs from under him and lowered him to the floor. The heat from the log burner reached my face, and déjà vu skirted around the edge of my conscious thoughts, taking me back to when I'd met Kim, to that hazy day at the festival I'd fought tooth and nail to avoid. I'd been a different man since that day, like Kim's touch had set me on a path I'd desperately needed to travel, perhaps my own recovery of sorts.

Could he taste the wine on my tongue? Alarmed by the thought, I pulled back, but Kim restrained me, holding me tight against him, his kiss fierce and demanding, his long legs wrapped around my waist like a cage.

And I knew then that I wasn't getting off this train.

I slowly opened my eyes. Kim's gaze was searching. Frightened. "Don't go."

"I won't. I'm right here, I promise."

For a moment I feared he hadn't heard me, but then Red's lips brushed my neck again, and the lightness of her touch seemed to reach Kim's face.

"Beautiful boys," she whispered. And I sensed her ghost around us and settle on the couch. Her presence was comforting . . . reassuring where perhaps many people would've found it intrusive. I looked at her and she smiled, and the heat between Kim and me cast a glow about the room that even the brightest flame couldn't match.

I moved so my body covered Kim completely, and kissed him, absorbing his quiet moan like it was my own, and sliding my tongue against his. His slender legs tightened around me, and he tugged me closer, tilting his head so our kiss deepened.

But I couldn't resist a glance at Red. Beside us on the couch, she shifted, leaning back, her hourglass body a picture of relaxation. Somewhere along the line she'd lost Kim's T-shirt, leaving her in just her shorts, and the kind of bra I'd dreamed about as a conflicted teenager.

She flashed me a wink that made my cock harder, and then Kim moaned, bringing my attention back to him. He loosened his legs around me, and let them fall open, his intentions suddenly clear, and it was *this* that finally shocked me, despite having sensed from the beginning that he was a versatile lover.

I stripped us both of jeans, socks, and underwear, and lay over him once more, pressing us together like I'd never been gone. His dick was as hard as mine—harder—and the temptation to straddle him and sink down on his cock was strong, but I didn't. Instead, I moved over him, nudged his legs wider apart, and pushed them back to his chest. Condoms and lube appeared like magic, pressed into my palm by a hand I barely noticed as Kim sank his teeth into my neck.

He broke away with a growl. "Fuck me."

I didn't need telling twice. I rolled a condom on and lubed up, my eyes drifting to Red, who was watching us with a hooded expression I couldn't entirely read. It felt almost natural to ask her to join us, though in what capacity, I didn't quite know.

Like she'd heard my errant, rambling thought, Red shook her head with another devilish wink. *This isn't about me, sweetheart.*

And it wasn't. It was about Kim, and me, and Red—about all of us, perhaps. Maybe. Who the fuck knew?

Not me, but as I slid slowly inside Kim, it didn't seem to matter. It was obvious that Red was getting off on seeing us together, and there was nothing in her gaze but a heated kindness that made everything right, filling the gaps in the foundations Kim and I had fudged since we'd met.

I looked down at him. His head was thrown back, his eyes closed, already lost to me fucking him, and my heart skipped a beat. Christ, he was stunning. I cupped his jaw in my hand and thrust into him, a ragged groan escaping me. How had I not dreamed of this . . . of the tight, wet heat of him clamped around me? Of his blunt nails digging into my hips? What the fuck had we been doing all this time when we could've been doing this?

"Jas."

Kim tensed and I quickened my pace, arching my back as his heels drove me deeper into him. He moaned and warmth pulsed between us, coating our stomachs. His body clamped tighter around me, and I knew I was about to become beautifully and wonderfully undone.

I mourned the loss of the magic that sealed us together, even as release rushed up on me, searing through me until I was devoid of all else. I dropped my head and groaned, seizing up and shuddering as I came.

Still groaning, I dug my teeth into Kim's chest, and I lost myself to his embrace, sweat and cum mingling, our breathing so laboured I couldn't tell where his ended and mine began.

Damn, I was tired, wrecked, but conversely too wired to close my eyes, and too enchanted by Kim to reclaim the hold he had on me. And so we stared at each other, unblinking, chests heaving, until Red placed a warm flannel on the back of my neck.

"Clean up. He's not going anywhere."

I took her word for it and detached myself to clean us up and ditch the condom. When I returned, I found him as I'd left him, smiling and drowsy, what little un-inked skin he had stained with an entrancing flush.

Drawn to him, I lay down beside him, dragging a gentle kiss over his jaw. "You okay?"

Kim hummed. "I'm wrecked."

The echo of my own sentiment made me grin. The floor of his trailer was surprisingly comfortable, and I couldn't imagine ever moving.

Red draped a blanket over us. I forced myself to look away from Kim and saw that she was dressed again.

"Don't go." She seemed surprised. I held out my hand. *"Stay."*

The conflict in her eyes was clear to see, and Kim, who'd said very little since I'd stumbled into his home, finally stirred. "Let her go, Jas."

Whether it was the way he said my name—the low tone that made me shiver—or something in his eyes that only she could see, I had no idea, but the standoff was brief. Red gave a gentle shake of her head and left the room.

She came back with more blankets and put another log in the burner. I wanted her to look at me again, but she didn't. She kissed Kim's cheek and left, and then Kim and I fell asleep, tangled together like we'd lain like this our whole fucking lives.

CHAPTER
ELEVEN

The tickle of sunlight on my face woke me the next morning. My hips hurt from being curled on the floor, and my shoulder was bent at an odd angle, but Christ, Kim's arms around my waist felt good.

It seemed criminal to move, but curiosity got the better of me. I shifted slowly onto my back and found Kim fast asleep. For a fleeting moment, it slipped my mind that the empty space behind him meant something. I touched his face, recalling the ethereal strain in him the night before when he'd come.

I'd never seen anything more beautiful, but as entranced as I was, Kim's peaceful silence set my attention drifting, and now I remembered Red, and the rueful hope in her eyes as she'd watched Kim and me add a primal brick to our foundations.

Carefully, I disentangled myself from Kim's addictive embrace and glanced around. A scrawled note by the burner caught my eye, and I reached over Kim to snag it. The note smelled of Red, though her handwriting was almost as illegible as my own.

Boys,

I'm hitting the road, and I won't be back anytime soon.

Be good. Be kind. And thank you. Your love is beautiful, and I've learned more from you than you'll ever know.

Lena xx

There was a cryptic message in there somewhere, but Kim stirring kept me from brooding over it. He opened his eyes, and I handed him the note. "She's gone."

He nodded, still blinking away sleep. "I thought she might."

"Yeah?"

"Yeah." He sat up. "She didn't just come back for me, but I know she stayed so long because she was waiting for the moment I didn't need her anymore."

"But you'll always need her."

I believed that as much as Kim, maybe more, but he shook his head. "She's got her own life—her own...entanglements. And something solidified that when I met you. It's like this —" he gestured between us "—whatever it is, has set her free."

Could matters of the heart be so kind? Unwelcome, Rich's belligerence when he'd been caught flashed into my mind. The cynic in me had sought strength from it, vindication, but as Kim's theory sank in, I realised that perhaps I wasn't as jaded as I liked to believe.

Kim lay down again, tugging me with him. "I like sleeping on the floor. Makes me feel young."

"Young? I feel fucking battered. You're gonna have to show me your bed one of these days."

"It's over there." Kim jerked his head at the couch. "Pulls out to a tasty king-size when I remember to do it."

I frowned. "So what's in the back, then?"

"A mess, mainly, but it's where I do painting and stuff—canvas, not wood. Ink designs that never make it to skin. I've got some of Brix's work in there, and Calum's."

Calum. I'd heard the name a few times now. Brix Lusmoore's…boyfriend, maybe? "Can I see?"

"See what? A bunch of old paintings and a pile of tarpaulin?"

"Yes."

"You're fucking weird." Kim got up anyway, grumbling, and led me to where the back of the trailer merged with the extension.

The space was brighter than I'd imagined, helped along by the stark white walls and large windows I hadn't seen before as they were on the opposite side to the orchard entrance. I looked out over the miles of fields. In the distance, lay Belly Acre Farm, and beyond that, the moody blue sea, shimmering on the horizon above Porth Ewan's cliffs. The view was stunning, inspiring, and only the insatiable desire to see Kim's artwork tore me away.

And fuck, what artwork. There wasn't as much as he'd led me to believe, just a handful of abstract paintings that had his block-like signature, but they were all stunning—full of tempestuous colour and chaos. One in particular drew me in to the point that Kim waved his hand in front of my face.

"Have it, if you like," he said. "It'll only end up on the bonfire."

"On the bonfire?"

"I burn all my paintings."

I opened my mouth. Shut it again. "Why?"

Kim shrugged. "They don't come from a good place."

My heart ached for him as I imagined the cloud of distress lurking behind each piece. Art therapy? Maybe. Whatever it was, the paintings would haunt me long after Kim had burned them on his fire.

"Don't go," Kim whispered.

The echo of Kim's plea the previous night brought me back to the present, but his expression was playful now, devoid of the fear that had lanced my chest then. "Huh?"

Kim smiled a little. "My old man says I have the attention span of a drunk fish, but you take the piss, mate."

It was an accusation I'd faced before, though it wasn't entirely accurate. My attention span was fine; I just rarely focused where I should. "Are you working today?"

"Yeah. Studio first, then the workshop."

"How many days do you work there?"

"A couple, give or take, depending on how much I've got on."

I thought of the ever-growing list of work my family was demanding from him. "I'm surprised you have any spare time at all, to be honest."

Kim grimaced. "I haven't, really. I only took yesterday off because I thought Lena was going to leave."

"And you were right."

"First time for everything, eh? Are you hungry? I've got to swing by the workshop before eight if I've got any hope of staying on schedule, but I've got time for a buttie."

Eight? I checked my phone and saw it was barely seven. Damn. It had been a long while since I'd been awake and functioning so early in the day, and beyond being hungry, I was bloody *starved*, a typical hangover from a Manning family dinner. "Tell you what, I'll stay for breakfast if you let me cook. I can't remember when I last ate a hot meal that hadn't been cooked for me by someone else."

"That's kinda sad, bro. What do you live on?"

"Nothing you need in your life, *bro*."

I retreated to Kim's tiny kitchen and set about buttering bread and frying bacon while he took a shower. A fruitless search for HP sauce took me to the fridge, where an envelope balanced behind a Bob Marley magnet caught my eye. It had my name on it. Intrigued, I reached for it, but as Kim's footsteps sounded behind me, I stuffed it in my pocket. I'd recognised the scrawl as Red's, and something told me she'd left the envelope separate from her goodbye note for a reason.

A reason that seemed unimportant as Kim wove his long, warm arms around me. "Watcha cooking?"

"Bacon. That all right? You said you wanted a buttie."

"Can't go wrong with a bacon sarnie. Did you find the ketchup?"

"No, but to be fair, I was looking for HP."

Kim pulled a face. "You like that shit? Why? You ain't northern."

"Southerners eat brown sauce too."

"Not this one." Kim retrieved the sauces while I loaded buttered farmhouse bread with crispy bacon. Breakfast of champions, and gone far too soon.

We polished them off in record time. I offered to wash up, but Kim refused. "I'll do it later. What are you doing now? Are you driving home, or into town?"

My wobble-bike adventure came flooding back. "Actually, do you think I could cadge a lift? I kinda cycled here last night."

"Cycled?" Kim peered out of the window. "On what? I can't see a bike."

Shit. I couldn't quite recall where I'd dumped Gaz's bike.

Kim helped me search the outskirts of the commune, and eventually, we discovered the bike upside down in a ditch.

"It's got a flat tyre," Kim observed. "You won't be able to ride it anywhere."

"I didn't do much riding last night. It was more of a scoot."

Kim chuckled. "I've got some tyres at the shop. I'll bring a couple home later if you're okay leaving it here?"

I couldn't imagine that Gaz would be missing it, so I left it by Kim's front door and clambered into the pink Ford to cadge a lift into town. Kim didn't say much on the drive and we were on my doorstep before I remembered I'd never told him where I lived.

Kim shrugged when I said as much. "It's a small town. Everyone knew when a fit bloke moved into number twelve."

"Fit?" I scoffed. "Speak for yourself."

"I do." Kim backed the Ford into a space that was hardly big enough for a go-kart. "Where's your car?"

Fuck's sake. It was exactly where I'd left it at the farm. I admitted my idiocy with a groan and covered my face with my hands. Kim laughed. "Booze makes you scatty, eh?"

"Not really. I'm as much of a knobhead without it."

Kim laughed harder. "Do you want me to run you back there?"

"Nah. I don't need it. I'll get it later."

"Fair enough." Kim put the Ford in gear and his hand hovered over the handbrake. "So . . ."

"So." I made no move to get out of the car. Kim and I had made no verbal commitment to each other from this point on, but I couldn't let him go without knowing when I'd see him again.

"Do you wanna come over later?"

Relief poured through me, seeping from my brain into every nerve. I turned to Kim and smiled. "Later?"

He shrugged. "I've got a mad day, but I've got to come

home sometime, right? Would be fucking ace if you were there . . . I mean, if you haven't got shit to do of your own."

I did have shit to do. Working for myself was a train I could never get off, but Kim knew that better than anyone, and the promise of an evening with him was likely all the motivation I'd need to get my arse in gear anytime before midnight. "I can probably get there around eight. That cool?"

"Aye-aye. If I'm late, let yourself in. I never lock up."

The Londoner in me shuddered, but my parents hadn't seen their house keys in years—it was the Porth Ewan way. Besides, Kim's lax security wasn't the point. Last night had been magical, but in all the heady distraction of topping Kim, I'd neglected to say the one thing he'd likely needed to hear the most. "Kim, I'm sorry."

He frowned. "What for?"

"For making you feel like shit. I never meant to. It was just, hard, you know? I'd kind of set myself up to be a terminal bachelor, and then I met you, and my brain exploded—"

Kim silenced me with a kiss. "Jas, it's fine. I get it, I really do. You aren't the only one who wasn't set up for something like this."

There was so much more to say, and I wanted to throw myself at his feet, beg his forgiveness for ever making him feel like he wasn't good enough for the flimsy commitment I'd offered him so far, but a firmness in his gentle smile silenced me. He so fucking clearly didn't want to hear it.

With a rueful sigh, I kissed his cheek, lingering over his unshaven jaw, breathing in the clean, woody scent that was uniquely him. The booze I'd drunk the night before was long gone, but I still felt drunk . . . drunk on life, on sex, on *him*. Only the knowledge that the sooner I left him, the sooner I'd see him again, drove me to haul myself out of the ridiculous car.

I watched him disappear into the distance, my chest warm and tight, the memory of sinking my cock into him eclipsing everything else that had happened.

God.

The craving to just be in his company was all-consuming, but the desire to fuck him again was something else—something that I could lose a whole day to if I didn't get moving. Was it truly so hard to tear myself away from my dirty daydreams?

Apparently so, but I did it anyway. A bucket of coffee called my name, and I spent the rest of the day prepping for my next job and doing the mountain of admin I'd been avoiding. I was on my way for a much-needed shower when I remembered Red's envelope, stuffed and crumpled into the back pocket of my jeans.

Jeans that I'd ditched on my bedroom floor.

Naked, I padded back to retrieve them, and the envelope slipped free as I picked them up. I slung them onto my bed, caught the envelope before it hit the floor, and turned it over in my hands. It smelled of Red—of musk and sunshine—and I tore it open with a pounding heart.

> *Jas,*
>
> *I'm going to try and say what I meant to say the first time we spoke, though to be honest, I feel like we met a long time ago . . . perhaps we did, but I digress.*
>
> *Kim means the world to me. For many years he <u>was</u> my world. I lived for him, and him for me. But life went on around us, and things changed. We changed.*
>
> *Do you believe in the stars, Jas? Because I do, and I saw them align when you and Kim came*

*together at that gig. Like you need him as much as I
know he's always needed you.*

*Don't let the past, or even the present, cloud your
destiny. Let yourself be happy.*

*And take care of my boy. You both deserve it. I
won't ever be a stranger, but you probably won't see
me for a while, and that's for the best.*

*I love you both, even if you don't believe that yet,
Lena xox*

Wow. I folded the letter with exaggerated care and tucked it into the envelope. Red's words had been much as I'd imagined they would be, but I was unprepared for the emotion ripping through my soul.

I sank onto the edge of my bed and sat on my shaking hands. Kim's bond with Red was nothing new, but the faith she'd placed in me by entrusting me with her most precious thing made my heart beat so fast I felt sick. Because Kim was fast becoming my most precious thing too, and I couldn't shake the sensation that I didn't quite deserve him.

CHAPTER
TWELVE

The shadow of self-doubt niggled at me well into the evening, to the point where I even shut down my computer and cleaned the flat—something I never did unless Laura was coming round.

By six o'clock, the place was spotless, and I set off for the farm. Taking advantage of one of autumn's rare warm nights, I walked through town, pausing to shoot the odd long exposure down the beach, chasing the setting sun. My luck ran out as I turned inland, though, and it began to rain. The nice kind of rain first, pleasant and refreshing, then big fat drops fell from the sky and soaked me to the skin.

Laura rushed out to meet me when she spied me traipsing up the mud-slicked drive. "You should've called. Your brothers could've driven the car into town."

It hadn't occurred to me to ask, but I was grateful for the towel and cup of tea Laura thrust into my hands once she'd got me inside. "How's the barn coming along?"

"Much the same as it was yesterday," Laura said dryly. "Though we had a visitor this afternoon. Honestly, I don't know how Kim does it. He must work day and night."

"Doesn't everyone?"

Laura sighed. "Everyone we know, I suppose. I think your dad will die with a spade in his hand."

It wasn't hard to imagine. Belly Acre Farm was my father's lifework, and I'd been raised to believe that his—and Laura's—work ethic was how life should be.

Until I met Kim.

The heat in my cheeks caught Laura's eye almost before I'd sensed it myself. She pinched me with a smirk that wouldn't have looked out of place on Gaz. "Do I take it that you're not here for your dinner?"

Despite the lingering disquiet in my veins, I couldn't help but grin back at her. "Nah. I'm just here for the car."

"Hot date?"

"I hope so, but I'm okay with anything warm."

Laura beamed and opened the fridge. She pulled out a giant Tupperware box and pushed it against my chest. "Casserole, in case you don't get round to cooking."

"Love you, ma."

I took the Tupperware and escaped to my car, still flushed like a motherfucker, anticipation fighting for dominance with affection for my lovely step-mother.

The drive to the commune took barely ten minutes, a far cry from my hooligan bike ride the night before. I drifted through the orchard, buzzing at the prospect of seeing Kim. A few people lingered outside their trailers, cooking over open fires now the rain had eased. Some waved, some nodded and smiled. Most paid me no heed, like Kim had nighttime visitors all the time. Perhaps he did.

Stop it.

I silenced the devil on my shoulder, a leftover gremlin that Rich had so kindly left behind. I believed in Kim and me with every day that passed, and I'd be fucked if I'd wreck it with the crazed paranoia I'd run all the way to Porth Ewan to escape. Red was right: Kim deserved better than that—we both did.

Shame he wasn't home. My knock went unanswered, and after a brief wait, I opened the trailer door to empty space and silence.

Disappointment surged through me, my craving for Kim at an all-time high, but there was little I could do but stick Laura's Tupperware in his tiny fridge and search for some entertainment while I waited for him. I ended up in the back room, camera in hand, lanterns lit. It truly was a beautiful space, and I entertained myself taking macro shots of the bristles of Kim's used paintbrushes.

And that was exactly how he found me a few hours later. "I'm so fucking sorry. I had no idea it was so late, or I'd have called."

In truth, I'd lost track of time too, and I'd given up checking my phone when it had become obvious that it wasn't going to ring. "Don't worry about it. I found something to do."

"So I see." Kim dropped his bag on the floor and ventured closer to peer over my shoulder. "Is that lens one of the close-up whatsits?"

"A macro? Yeah. Wanna see?"

"Damn right."

I passed Kim the camera and tried not to get a boner over how good my two favourite things looked *together*. "What do you think?"

Kim lowered the camera and blinked. "That's some crazy shit. It looks like tie-dyed hay."

"Cool, eh?"

"As cool as you are."

I snorted. "Not very, then. Gaz has been calling me an anorak my whole life."

"Gaz is a dick."

"There is that." I reclaimed my camera, turned it off, and set it aside. "A lovable one, though. Both my brothers are. Can't stand them, but I'd never be without the daft twats."

"I have mates like that."

"Makes me glad to be a loner. How was your day?"

"Long." Kim ran a hand through his hair with a weary sigh. "Inking and sanding . . . think I'll be doing both in my sleep tonight."

"Can we do it together?"

Kim's face brightened. "You're staying?"

"If you'll have me."

"I'm going to fucking have you, Jas. Make no mistake about that."

And have me he did. It was gone midnight by the time we peeled ourselves from the floor and dove into Laura's casserole. "Are you going to the autumn fair next week?"

Kim glanced up from slicing the best-looking sourdough loaf I'd ever seen outside London. "I was supposed to be, but I don't think I'll make it now."

"Why not?"

"I need every minute to make the barn opening."

Guilt burned a path to my gut. I set my fork down. "Have we asked too much of you? It won't be the end of the world if everything's not ready on the day. No one will have died."

"Except me, of embarrassment. I made your dad a promise. Besides, he's paying me a lot of money to get it right. I can't let him down."

I hadn't paid much attention to how much anything in the barn was costing, least of all the furniture, because I knew my dad well enough to know he'd have paid Kim a fair price for his work. But in the same vein, my father was so laid-back that Laura often joked that he waltzed through life horizontal. Swinging jokes aside, it was hard to imagine that he'd get on Kim's case about deadlines. Who cared if a few chairs turned up a few days late?

Kim cared. . . enough to push his food away and tug at his scruffy hair. "I'm on track, but the thought of falling behind keeps me up at night."

"It shouldn't." I cupped his chin and coaxed him to look at me, taking in the suddenly obvious lines of fatigue on his face. "Trust me, my dad would rather cancel the whole thing than know you were working yourself into the ground."

Kim's scepticism shone clear, and there wasn't much I could do to ease the stress from him except nudge him to finish his dinner.

After, I washed up while he dried. "I'm taking a day off tomorrow," I said. "Burnout, you know?"

Kim dropped cutlery into a drawer. "I thought we were done with that conversation?"

There was no malice in his tone, but I studied him anyway. "I'm talking about me. I've worked every day for weeks, and I'll chuck my computer out the window if I don't stop soon."

"At least you can stop."

"Only because I make myself, because I know the consequences if I don't."

"Yeah? Sent your PC flying before, have you?"

"It was a Mac, but yeah. I've had a few expensive temper tantrums."

Kim grinned, which was a relief. But part of me still wanted to shake him into taking me seriously. "I can see that, actually," he said. "You've got a wild streak in you."

The wildest side Kim had seen of me was with my clothes

off, but I let him have that one, especially when I remembered that he'd seen what I'd done to my Hoxton flat. I'd let him have anything to see him smile. "Anyway, I know you're busy, but do you want to do something? Lunch? A walk? A drive? There's some shots on the moors I want to get now the weather's gone all gloomy again."

"Shots? Thought you were taking a day off?"

"I am."

"Don't sound like it."

I poked my tongue out and flicked water at him. Soapy drops hit his face and clung to his jaw.

"Oh yeah?" He grabbed my wrists and spun me round, backing me against the sink, his face—his mouth—an inch from mine. "Don't tease me with that tongue. Drives me fucking mad, no matter how knackered I am."

A shiver ran through me. I licked my lips, absorbing Kim's low growl. "I won't have to tease you if you give me a straight answer. Want to do something tomorrow, or not?"

"Man, I'd love to spend the day with you, doing all the shit you just said, and more, but I gotta work, Jas. I told you; I can't stop."

I can't stop.

Everything about those three words was fucking unhealthy, but the sense of unease that had been so strong only moments ago was fast eclipsed by Kim's hips grinding against mine. In the haze of his lips on my neck and a growing boner, I struggled to blurt out a response before the power of speech deserted me. "Fuck it. I'll come to work with you. Now, are you going to show me your bed, or what?"

The next day found me trailing Kim around his workshop, shoving my camera in his face, and asking him a million questions he didn't have time to answer. Though, to be fair, he put up with it with an easy smile.

Midmorning, I brought him some tea. "Am I getting in the way? You can say if I am; I won't be offended."

"You're fine." Kim barely glanced up from his work. "Don't think anyone round here is going to complain about having a tea fella in for the day."

That, I could believe. "Still, not helping much, am I?"

"I don't need you to help. Your company is keeping me sane."

I nodded slowly. Kim's mood was becoming tough to gauge, but it was obvious that he enjoyed his work, even if he did have far too much of it. I *did* feel more than a little guilty for my part in his fatigue, though. We'd gone to bed at a touch before midnight, but it had been gone two before we'd found sleep.

Like he'd heard my thoughts revisit those heady few hours spent in his bed, Kim looked up and met my eye with a grin that lightened the fevered atmosphere of the workshop. His smile was like a warm breeze.

I love him.

Stop it.

But I did.

Around midday, I retreated to make the lunch run. The workshop was due a wood delivery to finish the final batch of chairs for the barn, and my car was in the way.

I drove to the seafront and went to the sandwich shop beside Blood Rush. My sleep-deprived body craved a pasty, but I didn't have the patience for the queues. Instead I ordered enough doorstep chicken sandwiches for a small army and stepped outside for some air while they were made.

Curiosity drew me to the studio's window. They'd changed the photographs, swapping out the vintage images for brighter, bolder shots of the resident artists: Brix, Kim, Calum, Lee, and Corey. Each artist had their own style, but there was a harmony running through the images that drew them all together.

"Can I help you?"

I turned to face the petite woman who'd emerged from the studio. It took me a moment to place her as the sole female artist in Blood Rush's window of fame.

Lee.

"Brix around?"

"Nope. Him and Calum are off today." The woman lit a cigarette and regarded me with a piercing gaze. "You're Kim's fella, ain't ya?"

"I'm Jas, if that helps."

"Not really. I knew that already."

Okay. I turned my attention back to the window. "Which work is yours?"

I waited for Lee to point to the dark geometric designs that seemed to suit her intensity. Her jerked nod at the delicate watercolour pieces caught me off guard, but what the fuck did I know? "They're gorgeous," I said. "I feel like I've seen that one before."

Lee followed my finger to the seahorse design at the back of the display. "You probably have if you've been hanging around Kim's place. Brix bullied me into painting it a few months ago, and it's on Kim's bathroom door."

Of course it was. I'd seen it this morning when I'd stumbled into the shower, but Lee was gone before the heat of that reached my cheeks, and the girl from the sandwich shop called me inside a moment later.

I drove back to the workshop with my giant bag of sandwiches, hoping it would persuade Kim to take a break before I left him to it for the rest of the day. A tough ask, but the signs of burnout in him were strong, and there'd been times in my life that would've been a whole lot easier if some fucker had just brought me a sandwich.

But when I pulled up outside the workshop, it quickly became clear that no picnic was going to fix Kim's day. I got out of my car and approached where he was standing, glaring, by a huge pile of what smelt like rotten wood. "What the fuck?"

He sighed. "You can say that again. What a crock of arse."

I picked up a damp plank of wood. It was soft, like a stale biscuit. "What happened?"

"I get wood from a social project over near Dartmoor Prison. They get the lags to collect it and bag it up, then I buy it, and the funds go to art projects or some shit. They're usually really good, but this lot must've got rained on. No good for nothing now."

"You can't send it back?"

"To a charity? Nah. Ain't got it in me, mate."

I couldn't think of a sensible solution, and from the slump of Kim's shoulders, neither could he. "Is there nowhere you can get more wood from?"

"Today?" Kim shook his head. "The only way is to collect it ourselves, but even if I pull all the guys from the workshop, it'll take all day, and we don't have the time to lose."

"I can help? The guys can keep working and—"

"Thanks, but you and me can't bring in enough on our own."

"No one else can help?"

Kim shrugged, and the problem was obvious. There were people who could—who would—help; he just didn't want to ask. "Brix is off today. Calum too. Why don't you call them?"

"How d'you know what Brix is up to?"

"Lee told me."

"Yeah? What else did she tell you?"

"Nothing. I got the feeling she didn't like me."

"Don't mind her. She's a spiky motherfucker, but she's got a good heart."

That was something I'd have to see to believe. "All your friends seem nice. Why won't you ask them for help?"

Kim shrugged. "They help me enough already."

"How?"

"How do you think?"

"I don't think anything. That's why I'm asking."

Kim sighed again and kicked a lump of wood. "It ain't easy to ask folk to help you when they've spent years carrying your sorry arse. I wouldn't have a home if it wasn't for Brix, or Lena. He gave her half the studio when I'd screwed up so bad we had nothing. She gave it back last year, but how the fuck am I supposed to ask him to collect driftwood on the beach for me when he's already given me so much?"

I had no answer to that, and not for the first time, it struck me that I had much to learn about Kim and the effect his addiction had on his day-to-day life, even when he was dry. "Look, I'm not going to pretend that I know how all this makes you feel, but the way I see it, you have two choices: ask your friends for help, or tell my dad you're going to be late. Whatever you do, you've got to reach out to someone, and there's no shame in that. You're human, not a fucking machine."

The last sentence came out harsher than I'd intended, and Kim raised a brow. "You sound like Lena."

"Good. She had your back, now I've got it. So what are you going to do?"

Being late was apparently not an option, so Kim called Brix, who turned up at the workshop ten minutes later, with a man I presumed to be Calum.

Brix greeted me with a nod. "I'll walk with you, if you want? Cal's better with Kim when he's in this mood."

Fair enough. Brix drove his van down to the beach, and we set to work collecting sand-dried driftwood. Like Kim, Brix didn't say a lot, but I enjoyed his company, and devoured every insight of Kim he let slip.

Not that he told me much that I didn't already know, something I voiced, by accident—thinking out loud—when we came to a stop by the rocks.

"Ah, I see." Brix glanced behind us to where Kim and Calum were dragging huge lumps of wood back to the van. "You're trying to figure out how to handle him, aren't you?"

"Handle him? Nah, I just don't know how to be there for him when he's like this."

Brix said nothing for a moment, focusing instead on shoving wood into the sack he carried. Then he straightened up and fixed me with a gaze that was a disarming mix of hope and sadness. "Kim's a proud man. I don't often know he's been down until after the event. All I can say is keep him as close as he'll let you, and don't blame yourself if his demons get him anyway. You can't control that shit any more than he can."

"He told me he's fucked everyone over at one time or other."

Brix snorted. "It's never gone down like that. The only help he's had has been forced on him. He's a bugger like that, and it drives me up the wall. Which is why I leave him with Cal. That man's got the patience of a saint."

The love in Brix's gaze then made me feel like I was intruding on a private moment, even though Kim and Calum were too far away to feel the weight of Brix's warm words.

We completed the rest of our wood forage in relative silence, catching up with Kim and Calum at the van.

Calum approached me with a shy grin. "I think we've got enough. Brix is going to drive it back with Kim. Fancy a pint?"

I couldn't imagine anything better, but guilt gnawed at my gut. Where was Kim's relief? His quiet half hour to think of nothing but beer and easy conversation—

"Go." Kim elbowed me in the ribs. "I'll find you later."

"You sure?"

"Sure enough to deck you if you don't do as you're told."

His tone left no room for argument, though the playful glint in his eye held a promise he'd make good on later. And I couldn't deny that it felt good to see his easy light return.

Calum and I decamped to the Sea Bell, a pub that the Porth Ewan locals claimed as their own.

"I still feel kinda weird in here," Calum confessed. "Even when Brix is with me, they still look at me like I'm in my birthday suit."

"That doesn't change. If you weren't born here, you'll always be an emmet."

Calum chuckled. "True that."

We bought pints and sat outside, despite the bitter breeze the ocean had kicked up since we'd left the beach. Calum was quiet, but it was different to the reticence that Kim and Brix carried like a second skin. Instead it seemed to be shyness that I hoped would fade as we sat together.

And fade, it did. Like me, Calum was a London boy, and it turned out that a similar clusterfuck had led us both home to Porth Ewan.

"So your ex was an arsehole too?"

Calum nodded. "Something like that. He did me a favour in the end, though. I'm never going to be a native around here, but I'm more at home than I've ever been."

I seconded that, though it was obvious Calum's content-ment stemmed from his relationship with Brix—that he'd have been happy anywhere as long as they were together—and envy crept through me as he talked. Would I ever have that with Kim? I was *so close* to falling in love with him, indelibly marked by the short time we'd already shared, but would he ever look at me like Brix looked at Calum? Would he ever *trust me* enough to love me like that?

And what about me? I'd dragged all my shit down to Porth Ewan, never stopping to think that I'd meet anyone to share it with. Rich had hurt me badly, but I knew now that what I'd felt for him had been a long way from love, and light years away from how I felt about Kim.

I *loved* Kim, and the realisation struck deep. Pain lanced my chest . . . and my heart. I loved Kim, and it would never matter if he loved me back, because how I felt about him was *here*, on its own, and it wasn't going anywhere.

"Dude." Calum's dark gaze bore into me. "You've got it bad, eh?"

I didn't have it in me to deny it. Didn't want to. And I

didn't need to. Calum's shrewd grin told me he already knew what was going on in my tiny brain.

"Be patient," he said. "These Porth Ewan boys are born thinking they don't deserve to be happy, that anything good needs to cost blood, but they're wrong. We love them, whether they let us or not. Just gotta wait for them to see it."

Wise words, and I took them to heart as we found room for a few more beers.

That afternoon, I left my car at the workshop and raided the local shops for something to cook for dinner. Then I walked to the commune, musing that my relationship with Kim was fast becoming the most exercise I'd had in years, even without the fuck-hot sex.

In the trailer, Kim's bed—still rumpled from the night before—was tempting, but I put off a nap in favour of knocking up one of the only proper meals I could cook: Laura's fish pie.

It was resting on the side when Kim finally came home that evening. I met him at the bottom of the steps, offering an embrace that he all but fell into.

"You smell of lemons," he rumbled into my neck.

I laughed, with relief more than anything, because it was a hell of a lot better than reeking of fish. "Come inside. I made dinner."

"I don't know what to say," Kim said as I shoved a bowl of fish pie and peas his way. "It seemed too much to hope you'd be here when I got home."

"Where else would I go?"

"Home? Your parents? On the piss with Calum? I've been such an arse all day, I can't imagine why you'd want to be here."

"Then you need to work on your imagination. Now eat your dinner."

CHAPTER
FOURTEEN

The next few days were spent drifting between Kim's place and mine, juggling work and snatching a few hours with Kim when he wasn't holed up in the workshop. It was tough, with the barn opening creeping ever closer, and it wasn't long before I was as tired as him.

"Go home," he said to me on Saturday morning. "*Sleep*. I love having you here, but I know you've got as much on as I have."

That wasn't entirely true, but I couldn't deny that I had a backlog of admin to get through before I could start my next job. And I had a photography gig in Bristol that I had to prepare for, a two-night trip that I was dreading, despite the job being one I'd actively pursued. "Are you coming to the fair tomorrow?"

Kim shook his head. "I can't. I've got too much to do. Corey and Calum are going to run my stall for me."

"Corey?"

"From the studio."

"Oh."

I turned away, trying to hide my frustration. Jesus. When was this bloke going to see daylight again?

Kim caught my arm. "Don't be like that. I'm sorry, okay? I'm nearly done, I promise."

"I know," I said with a sigh. "I just fucking miss you."

Kim kissed me, silencing any negativity brewing in my veins, chasing it down, and eclipsing it with the devilish twist of his tongue. I fell against him, kissing him back, then pulled away, pressing my forehead to his.

"Don't forget to eat."

"I won't," he promised. "You too, though. I know how you get when you're busy. We're as bad as each other."

I let him have that one. "Maybe I'll see you tomorrow, after? If you finish in time."

"Yeah . . . maybe. I'll do my best."

It was as good as I was going to get for now. I left him to it and went home, hitting my desk with a focused fervour it had missed in recent days. Time slipped away from me, and it was dark when a knock at my door disturbed me hours later.

I ran to the door, hoping to find Kim, but it was Gaz, bearing an apron and a mischievous grin.

"You'll be needing this tomorrow."

"What the fuck for?"

"To run the stall with ma. The rest of us have to see in a delivery from your fella; last but one, apparently."

"And it takes all of you to see it in?"

"Unless you want lover boy to unload it on his own? You know Dad can't do it with his back."

Dick. I knew I was lucky that my family was so accepting of my sexuality, but that didn't make his shit-eating grin any less irritating, or the apron any easier to take. I booted Gaz out without offering him a beer, and skulked back to my computer. Stupid fucking fair. I'd been planning on photographing it and collating the images for the local magazine, not flogging chutney and jam. But I had no choice in the matter, and besides: there was no way I'd let Kim lug all those chairs to the barn on his own. If there was one thing my brothers were good for, it was hoofing shit around.

The next morning, I got up at the crack of dawn, which was easier than I'd have imagined without Kim's warm presence to keep me in bed. I spent a few hours finalising my prep for my Bristol trip—packing, checking train times, charging a million batteries, and loading the software I used for my specialist drone onto my tablet.

Then I tied my dodgy apron on and drove to the farm that was hosting the last outdoor fair of the year.

I found Laura already there and halfway set up. I helped her finish, then sloped off to find some breakfast. The smell of bacon lured me to a nearby stall and as luck would have it, past Kim's stand, manned by Calum and Corey.

Calum waved. I nodded back and shouted that I'd drop by later if I got the chance, which was unlikely judging by the queue of vehicles lining up to get into the fair.

Amazing.

It was midafternoon by the time warm arms slid around my waist, making me jump out of my skin.

"Jesus."

Kim laughed. "Man, you're such a dreamer. How have you never been mugged?"

"Piss off." I waved a sticky jam spoon at him. "Maybe no fucker sees much worth taking, eh?"

"I don't believe that."

Kim's gaze turned heated, and Laura cleared her throat, amused. "Boys, behave. Why don't you go and get a drink? I can manage here."

It was a kind offer, but there was no way I was leaving her

alone with the afternoon crowds. Besides, Kim had a stall of his own to check up on.

"Come for dinner after, then?" she asked Kim. "I've got enough lamb at the farm for the whole town."

I waited for Kim to refuse, like he'd refused everything all week, but he was no more immune to Laura's kindness than anyone else. He left me with a promise to see me at dinnertime.

Later that evening, I still half expected him not to show up, so I got a massive kick out of finding him at Laura's table with my dad. "Did you get all your work done?"

"Nope, but I've got seventy-two hours, right?"

My dad chuckled. "And then some. It doesn't matter if there's a few things missing, son. What you've delivered already is plenty."

Kim smiled with enough light that I nearly melted through the floor. "Jas said you'd say that."

"That's because we raised him to treat people like humans, not robots. If only he'd apply it to himself, eh?"

Fucking hell.

I retreated to the stove to irritate Laura while Dad and Kim talked shop, and it wasn't long before the rest of the world and his dog filed in for dinner.

The meal was loud and rowdy, the kind of occasion I usually endured, but with Kim beside me, his hand on my leg, *squeezing*, I enjoyed every moment. And if the amount of food Kim put away was anything to go by, he did too. I tried not to consider it an indication of how little he'd eaten while I'd left him to his own devices.

After dinner, my dad cracked out his homemade plum brandy. I took that as our cue to leave and hustled Kim outside.

In the yard, I pushed him against my father's Land Rover, hoping the taste of wine on my lips wouldn't upset him.

It didn't seem to. He kissed me back, then spun us around, slamming his body against me, pressing, grinding. "Come home with me?"

I groaned. "I *can't*. I've got to get home so I can drive to Truro in the morning."

"The Bristol thing?"

"Yeah." Regret punctured me. The best job I'd had since coming to Porth Ewan seemed like the worst idea in the world with Kim's cock digging into my thigh. "I've got to leave at eight."

"Eight, eh?"

"Yeah."

"That's plenty of time for what I've got in mind. Come on, let's go."

And by *go* he meant drive back to my place.

I let us in, almost shy as I dropped my keys in the bowl. No one outside of my immediate family had ever been inside my Porth Ewan flat. "This is me."

Kim glanced around. "Ain't got much here, have you?"

"I left it all in London, remember? In bits?"

Kim sent me a dark look and continued his inspection while I chucked our coats in the cupboard and went to the kitchen for Jammie Dodgers and mugs of herbal tea. What I wanted, but Kim's gaze was troubled with apology. You can have a nightcap if you want, you know. Don't deprive yourself on my account."

"I'm not. I live on this shit when Laura doesn't send me a care package."

"I don't believe you. That fish pie you made was awesome."

I laughed. "I'm glad you think so, because it's the only thing I can cook, and it's not something I'd ever cook for myself."

"You should cook for yourself. It's good for the soul."

"Yeah? Done much cooking this week?"

"Piss off."

I laughed again and let it go. The time for nagging had passed, and I wanted to go to bed with him—to sleep, as much as anything. I'd missed him last night, and I'd be missing him even more tomorrow.

After giving Kim a brief tour, I led him to my bedroom where I ditched the tea and set about stripping him. He returned the favour, and we crawled into bed, burying ourselves, hiding from the world as we reconnected in every way possible.

Kim took control, and I let him, giving myself to whatever he wanted. He turned me onto my side and gently raised my leg, slipping into me from behind. The position was intimate, tender. My eyes fluttered as I came with a quiet gasp and felt another piece of my heart give itself over to him.

My alarm woke me the next morning. I rolled over, searching for Kim, but found nothing but a cold space where he'd been the night before.

Disappointment flooded through me, though I wasn't altogether surprised. Despite the awesomeness we'd ended on yesterday, Kim hadn't been able to hide his agitation at being away from his work. And it was an agitation I understood, so how could I be angry with him?

I couldn't, and I wasn't. Just a few more days and it would all be over, and then we could get back to building what we'd started.

Bleary, I got up, showered, and left the house with the last of the Jammie Dodgers stuffed in my pocket. My train was on time, and before I knew it, I was halfway to Bristol, leaving Kim far behind.

The notion made my stomach churn and my heart skip a beat. We'd gone from a one-night hookup, to friends, and then friends that fucked, to being completely entwined with each other, and being without him, even for two nights, felt all wrong.

So wrong, that I was tempted to get off the train at Bodmin and head straight back home. But I didn't. Beyond the fact that we both had work to do, I still hadn't got around to telling Kim I was head over heels in love with him and barging into the workshop a few hours after I was supposed to be gone for two days seemed insane.

I made it to Bristol and checked into my hotel. A text waited for me.

Kim: *thinking of you*

Three simple words that eased the anxious gripe in my gut. I smiled and fired a message back.

Jas: *thinking of you too . . . and missing you.*

Missing him didn't come close to how I was feeling, but after waiting a moment for a reply I didn't really expect, I pocketed the phone and got on with my day.

The job was in the city, photographing the interior of a cathedral and taking aerial footage of the outside with my Phantom 4. I did the drone work first, and the flights took most of the day, only stopping when the light got away from me.

I packed up and headed back to the hotel, craving a hot

shower, a beer, and a greasy burger. The shower in my room provided instant gratification, and a grumpy hotel porter appeared with my dinner a while later. I didn't bother with the beer. Whatever Kim thought about it, being with him was good for my alcohol consumption, and I was feeling the benefits of drinking less already.

My early start caught up with me fast. I was dozing off when my phone rang sometime later.

Blinking, I reached for it, expecting Dad or Laura panicking about something ridiculous to do with the barn opening.

Kim's throaty chuckle took me by surprise. "Did I wake you?"

I sat up and squinted at the time: four minutes past midnight. Damn. It had been ten o'clock last time I'd checked. "A little. I don't mind, though. I was hoping you'd call."

"Yeah?"

"Yeah. I've missed you today. I wish you were here with me."

"Me too, and if you'd gone a day later, I could've been."

The lightness in Kim's tone was a clue, and it took me a moment to grasp what it meant. "You finished?"

"Yup. Delivered the last dozen chairs an hour ago."

"Wow." I couldn't mask the awe in my voice. The last I knew, Kim had been twenty-five chairs short of the forty-chair order, with just a pile of driftwood to help him along. The scale of what he and his crew of guys had achieved in such a short time was incredible. "I'm so happy for you. How do you feel?"

"Relieved. I didn't think we were going to make it, and we wouldn't have done except that your dad called me this morning and told me not to paint the last few chairs . . . to keep 'em natural with just a varnish. Saved me two days of fannying around."

"Thank God for my dad and his indecisiveness, eh?"

"Indeed. Anyway, enough about me. How are you? How was your day?"

"Long." I lay back on the bed and stared at the ceiling. "Drone flying is fun, but it's hard work, you know? Got to make sure I don't hit anything."

"Like a plane?"

"Only if a plane was about to clip Bristol Cathedral, but yes . . . planes, birds, buildings. I'm fucking knackered."

"Yeah, you sound it. I'm gonna let you get back to sleep."

"Don't go."

Kim chuckled softly. "I'm not going anywhere, mate. Get some shut-eye, yeah? And get through tomorrow. Then we can open that bloody barn and I can stop seeing it in my sleep."

Knowing that the sooner I slept, the sooner I'd be a day closer to seeing him again, I relented and whispered good-night. Kim returned the sentiment, but his soft sigh kept me from hanging up the phone.

"Hey. What is it?"

"Nothing, really, I just need you to know that I've never felt this way about anyone else. You believe that, don't you?"

I closed my eyes and pictured him on the steps of his beau-tiful trailer, long legs stretched out in front of him, nursing a cup of lukewarm tea. "I do. Goodnight, Kim."

"Night, Jas."

The next day passed in a blur of hard-core photography. I finished the aerial footage in the morning and set about the interior shots in the afternoon. I'd hoped to get it done by the evening, but it wasn't to be. Daylight faded too fast, leaving me stuck in Bristol for another night.

I called Kim to moan about it, but he didn't answer, and I

didn't call back. He hadn't had a night off in weeks and chances were he was fast asleep, catching up on the rest he'd so desperately needed. I sent him a text and passed out myself.

It wasn't until the next morning when I woke to a blank phone that I realised I'd left my charger at home. Going out to buy one would cost me precious time, so I didn't bother. I headed straight for the cathedral to finish my work as fast as humanly possible.

I wrapped it up in two hours and dashed to the station, jumping on the first train I saw heading south. It was barely ten o'clock, and the three-hour fast line left me plenty of time to make the four o'clock barn launch.

Or so I'd thought. Animals on the tracks meant delays, and I got caught in traffic on my way back to Porth Ewan. It was after five by the time I rushed up the driveway of Belly Acre Farm, and I'd missed the grand opening, though the party appeared to be in full swing.

"There you are!" Laura grabbed my arm and propelled me into the barn. "I've been looking for you everywhere."

"Sorry, ma. My train got stuck. How did it go?"

"See for yourself," Laura said. "I've got to get back to the kitchen."

She left me at the door. I grinned after her, pleased for her, proud of her, and proud of everyone who'd been involved in a project that had seemed like it would never come to fruition.

I stood to one side and surveyed the bustle of the packed barn: the families eating Laura's cake and Gaz's chutney with local cheese, the buzz of conversation, the hum of content-ment, and the faint surge of gentle laughter that warmed the barn even more than the central fireplace. And of course, the bespoke artisan furniture that Kim had poured his heart and soul into. I wandered around, taking in everything from the mismatched driftwood chairs, to the beautiful tables he'd built from piles and piles of discarded pallets. Each piece was stunning, and none were the same. For the millionth time since I'd met him, I was floored by his brilliance.

I was on my second loop when I spotted the picture frames hung on the walls—rustic white imperfect squares that I instantly knew had been made with the smashed-up bookcase from my London flat. Eight of them in total, all filled with a timeline of Manning family photographs. The sight of my family made my heart swell, and it was the first time in as long as I could remember that I felt something for a photo I hadn't taken myself.

A light came on in my soul, illuminating the giant space that Kim had carved out. All I needed now was the man himself, but there was no sign of him in the barn, not even with Brix and Calum, huddled up at the back, sharing cake.

"I haven't seen him in days," Brix said. "I thought he was with you."

"He was until Monday morning. I've been in Bristol since then."

Brix's concern was sudden, and the excitement I'd arrived with died an abrupt death. I looked at Calum, hoping to see the measured calm I'd seen in him on the day we'd gathered the driftwood, but he already had his phone in his hand. "I'll call around," he said. "Jas, go check he's not with your dad. Don't worry, if I find him, I won't make it obvious you're looking for him."

Kim getting the hump was the least of my concerns as I left Calum and Brix behind and made a loop of the farm, asking around, but no one had seen him.

My dad trailed me out of the farmhouse, his flowered shirt billowing behind him. "What is it, son? Has something happened?"

"I don't know. I just expected him to be here."

"He did say he would be. Maybe he's running late? Have you called him?"

"My phone's dead."

"Give it here. I'll plug it in."

I left my phone with my dad and rushed back to Brix and Calum, who were at the barn door.

"No one's seen him," Calum said, "but that doesn't mean anything's happened."

Brix looked less optimistic.

My frown deepened, taking my heart with it. "What are you thinking? Are you worried?"

"I'm always worried about Kim. Even the good stuff sends him off the rails."

My heart dropped into my stomach as Kim's ominous words about his past relapses flashed into my mind.

"I guess I'm a bit depressed. It happens now and then, especially when something good happens in my life. Weird, eh?"

He'd sounded happy the last time I'd heard his voice. Free. Was it possible that the relief of finishing such a mammoth job had tipped him over the edge?

By the obvious worry in Brix, I reckoned so. "I need to find him."

"He's not at home," Brix said. "I got Cam and Saint to check."

I had no idea who they were. And I didn't care. "Where else could he be?"

"The cliffs," Calum answered. "It's where they all go when they can't feel the sea."

The cryptic answer made perfect sense as I recalled the evening I'd spent with Kim huddled up in my car at Porth Ewan's highest point.

I made a run for my car, which I'd had to leave on the road leading up to the farm. Some twat in an Audi had blocked me in. I forced my way out and scraped the shit out of their fancy paintwork, then I hit the road, my heart still seeping from the soles of my feet. Much of Kim was still a mystery to me, but of one thing I was certain.

Something was wrong.

CHAPTER
FIFTEEN

I drove to the cliffs, taking way too many risks on Porth Ewan's batshit roads. As I drove, it began to rain—really rain—and big fat drops obscured my vision, forcing me to slow down in time for a wide truck to come at me from the opposite direction.

Slipping past was impossible. I skidded to halt, earning myself a finger from the truck driver. But I didn't give a rat's fuck.

I hit the accelerator again, the car lurching forward. The cliffs were still a mile away, but the ocean claimed the horizon, dark and angry, the sky fast catching up, and it fucking scared me—because I'd spent my whole life chasing the light.

And, because I was an *emmet*. Unless Kim had rocked up somewhere fucking obvious, I had no chance of finding him in the dark.

Fuck. Panic seized me, and I drove faster, pushing the car's one-litre engine to its limits until the road to the cliff-top car park finally came into view—a road that was blocked by the same motorbikes I'd seen around Red—around *Lena*. The same men astride them.

I slowed as one approached my window, and hit the switch to roll it down.

The biker stared back at me like he had the whole world on the tip of his tongue. But he said nothing and another took his place, pointing a gloved finger up the road.

"He's up there. Don't think he's gonna jump, but I've been wrong about that shit before."

Grief clouded the biker's dark eyes, but I didn't have time to give a shit. I drove around him and continued to the car park, hurling my car to a stop as I scanned the deserted space.

No cars. No people.

No Kim.

Maybe the bikers were wrong. Or Kim had left without them seeing.

Maybe he'd left *me*.

Or gone to Red.

Or...

Maybe he'd jumped and the bikers didn't see that either.

Sheer terror gripped me and I scrambled out of my car as lightning razored the sky, a flash of white that gifted me a better view of the dark clifftop.

Of the bench and the slumped figure huddled in the rain.

I ran, vaulting the low wooden fence as rain monsooned around me, soaking me to the skin with coldness I didn't feel.

"Kim." I reached him and dropped to my knees, taking his limp hand. "Hey. What's wrong? Can you look at me? Please?"

He didn't so much as twitch, and for the longest moment, I honestly thought he was dead.

Then he shifted, his hand fell from mine, and the only good thing about it was that I knew he was alive.

"Hey." I grabbed his hand again. "Whatever it is, I'm here, okay? But you need to get out of this rain before you get fucking pneumonia."

If he hadn't already.

I leaned over him, searching for another sign of life. I waited for the smell of booze to hit me—beer, wine, whiskey, I'd never asked him what his choice of poison was—but instead of alcohol, all I smelt was wood and rain.

All I smelt was him.

I put my hand to his cold cheek. "Kim."

My plea was whispered this time, but by some miracle seemed to penetrate where I'd already failed.

Kim groaned and his eyes fluttered open, bloodshot and unfocused. "Jas?"

"It's me. Can you sit up?"

Kim blinked. "What are you doing here?"

"Might ask you the same thing. It's wetter than an otter's pocket up here, and cold as fuck."

"Cold?"

The confusion in his troubled gaze tore me in two. I took both his hands in mine and tugged him forward, causing his feet to hit the ground. "We're up on the cliffs."

"The cliffs?"

"Yeah. You didn't show for the barn opening. I was worried. Calum told me to look for you here."

"Calum."

It wasn't a question this time, and slowly, cognition returned to Kim's green eyes.

He ripped his hands from me and covered his face again. "Fuck."

I rubbed his damp leg. "It's okay. We can fix it. How much did you drink?"

"Drink?" Kim dropped his hands like I'd burned him. "I didn't drink anything."

"No?" Stress sharpened my tone. "So why are you passed out on a bench in the rain?"

"I—" Kim glanced around. "Shit. How long have I been here?"

"I don't know. Do you remember coming up here?"

Kim nodded. "I came out for a walk."

"When you were drunk?"

"I'm not fucking drunk."

His shout was sudden and loud, even with the vicious wind swirling around us.

I reared back.

He caught my arm. "I'm sorry, I'm so sorry."

"Then tell me what happened. Please? I can't help if you don't."

His only answer was a violent shiver, reminding me that we were both wet through and exposed to the elements—him more than me, and Christ knew how long he'd been out here.

I coaxed him to his feet, steadying him as he wavered. "Come on. Let's get warm."

He didn't protest as I led him to my car.

I sat him in the passenger seat and slammed the door harder than I'd intended, helped along by the wind, then got in the driver's side.

Kim's head was down, his eyes closed. I touched his arm, rousing him. "Okay?"

"Where are we going?"

"Home."

And by that, I meant my place, where I knew where every drop of booze was, and could easily dispose of it the moment we walked through the door.

We made the journey in silence; me focused on the road, wondering how the bikers on their noisy rides had somehow vanished into thin air, Kim staring out of the window. If he was surprised to find himself at my flat a little while later, it didn't show. I steered him inside and helped him out of his wet clothes. "Shower. Warm yourself up. Don't lock the door, though, in case you fall."

"I'm not going to fall."

He drifted away before I could answer. I waited for him to slam the bathroom door, but he left it open and turned the shower on, and after a few minutes, I poked my head around the door to find him sitting in the bath, his face hidden in his knees.

The sight of him broke me, and the frustration I'd felt since the car park melted away if it had ever truly been there.

I joined him in the shower and turned the heat up to warm his bones. He didn't seem to notice me rubbing shampoo through his hair, even as I slid my fingers over his scalp to the base of his neck, kneading.

It was a while before his quiet sigh broke the silence.

"That feels nice."

"Good." I rose up on my knees, ignoring how my body naturally responded to being so close to Kim, and massaged his shoulders. "Enjoy it while you warm up. I'm usually too amorous around you to be this nice."

"You're always nice."

"Yeah? If that was true, perhaps I'd have known earlier that you needed me, eh?"

Kim looked up. "You weren't here."

"I know, and I'm sorry."

"No, that's not what I mean. I'd never want you to be—it's just—*Fuck*." Kim banged his head on the tiled wall behind him. "I called you a few times. Your phone was off."

"The battery ran out. I'm—"

"Jas, *please*. Don't be sorry for my bullshit. I can't handle that guilt on top of the rest of it."

With Kim apparently ready to talk, now seemed as good a time as any to steer him out of the shower and into my bed.

I slipped in beside him, clicking the TV on for some background noise before I turned to face him and gestured for him to pick up where we'd left off in the shower.

Kim's eyelids seemed to weigh him down. "What do you want to know?"

"Will you tell me what you drank?"

"I didn't drink."

"*Kim.*"

"I didn't, I swear. I wanted to, and kinda lost my mind over it, but I didn't drink. I promise."

Cynicism bubbled up my throat as I stared at him, warring with the reality that Kim had never lied to me before. That, despite his demons, he was so painfully honest sometimes that I wanted to weep. I believed him. I *had* to, or we had nothing. "So what happened?"

"What always happens, I guess." Kim stared down at his hands and traced the anchor tattoo on his index finger with his thumb. "I'm not good with downtime, especially when I'm on my own. I finished the barn job in the middle of the night, and no one was around—you, Lena. And the next day I had nothing to do either. It sounds fucking stupid. Like, why can't I read a book or some shit, or annoy Brix for the day? But it doesn't work like that. It gets louder and louder."

"And you want to drink to stop it?"

"I *always* want to drink, but it got out of hand this time because I had nothing and no one to distract me. I went mad with the power tools for a while, but then the generator failed, and I couldn't get hold of you, or anyone else, and then I felt like a selfish prick for even trying, so I took a few zopiclone, hoping I'd sleep it off."

"Zopiclone?" I searched my brain for where I'd heard the word before. "Sleeping pills?"

"Yeah . . . shit, don't look at me like that. I couldn't handle it, Jas. I needed to sleep."

His voice wavered. I slipped my arm around his slender shoulders and pulled him close, brushing his damp hair out of his face. He shivered. "Go on." I thumbed his cheek. "Tell me how you ended up on the cliffs."

"I don't know. The first pill I took didn't work, so I took another, and then one more. They must've kicked in all at once while I was walking. Good job I wasn't driving, eh?"

I felt sick. "You could've overdosed. Or got bloody pneumonia."

"I'd take that instead of this. Sometimes I think I'd rather have a fucking tumour."

There was no mirth in Kim's tone, only fatigue. I kissed him, then coaxed him to lie down with his head in my lap. Kim's addiction wasn't going anywhere, and neither was I. For now, that he was safe, warm, and in my arms was enough.

I tracked Brix down on Facebook while Kim slept, and called him. He seemed unsurprised to hear from me. I combed my fingers through Kim's hair as I filled Brix in on our cliff-top adventure. "He banged some Zopiclone, but he says he didn't drink."

Brix hummed. "If he says he didn't drink, then he didn't. He hides from us, but he doesn't lie. Mind, popping the sleeping pills isn't much better than hitting the sauce. It's still a chemical reaction to emotions he can't handle."

I couldn't argue with that, and I didn't try. "Do you think he needs Lena here?"

"No. Lena is gone, and it's how they both want it. If you're going to be with Kim, you need to learn to deal with this in your own way."

He was right, of course, and for that to happen, Kim and I had to talk again when he woke up, which sent a new flare of anxiety rippling through me. "He took three Zopiclone. Is that dangerous?"

"I wouldn't know, but I think the pills he has are the lowest dosage. Hang on, I'll ask Cal. He remembers numbers and shit."

Brix broke off to mumble to who I presumed was Calum, and my attention drifted to my bedroom window. It was raining again in earnest, and I couldn't help imagining Kim still passed out on that bench, soaked to the skin, and exposed to the bitter wind.

"...don't think he's gonna jump."

What if the mystery biker had been wrong? Or they hadn't found him, and I hadn't either?

Then what?

Brix saved me from answering that question. "Calum reckons Kim can take four of those pills before he hits the maximum dose, so he should be fine. Besides, he's probably already slept most of it off."

"I guess you're right."

"I have no idea if I'm right, Jas. But I know Kim won't want you worrying yourself to death. He doesn't wear guilt well. That shit fucks him up more than anything."

Don't I know it.

Though, as I thanked Brix and hung up, it struck me ironic that I'd learned as much about Kim today as I had in all the time I'd known him. And why was that? Kim talked, I just hadn't listened hard enough.

Kim slept right through until morning, while I watched, unable to close my eyes to the guilt and worry kicking up dust in my gut.

It was barely dawn when he woke. I slid down the bed to face him, cupping his cheeks with my palms. "Okay?"

Kim blinked slowly. "I think I need to go to a meeting."

"A meeting?"

"AA."

I nodded. "When and where? I'll take you."

"You don't have to do that."

"I know."

"But you're gonna?"

"Yeah."

Kim's wry half smile was the poor ghost of any grin I'd ever seen from him, but this morning, with the early morning light filtering through the curtains, it felt like the sun. "I'm sorry, Jas."

"Don't be. I'm here. I got you."

"Why?"

"Why do you think?"

Kim didn't seem to have an answer, and it wasn't the time for me to force my undying love on him. Instead, I got up and made tea, then drove him along the coast to Porth Luck, and the AA meeting held there every week.

I pulled up outside. Kim opened the door, but he didn't get out. "You don't have to take this crap on. We can go back to being friends anytime you want."

"What kind of friend would I be if I didn't support you in this?"

"A friend with better things to do than hang out at a dead-end church at dickhead o'clock in the morning."

"I'm not hanging out at the church. I'm going to sit in that fish shop across the road and eat my bodyweight in fried mackerel sandwiches. Unless you want me to come in with you?"

Kim shook his head. "Some meetings let you bring someone in. They don't like it here."

"Then I'll be just across the road. And, Kim?"

"Yeah?"

"I'll always be your friend, no matter what."

Kim's meeting took about an hour, so I made good on my promise to decamp to the fish shop.

The mackerel sandwiches came with tea.

Lots of tea.

I loaded up and opened my laptop, searching for something to do to occupy my tired brain. I toggled the Wi-Fi from my phone and logged into the enormous cloud storage that cost me a kidney in fees every month and opened a folder that contained more than a decade of unfinished personal projects.

More recently, there were a thousand shots of Kim, most of them taken at my old flat *before* we'd fucked on the floor, but there were others from before and after.

Frowning, I lined some up in chronological order, starting with the clandestine shot I'd taken of him that day I'd met him, and finishing with a playful pose he'd struck for me the day before I'd gone to Bristol. I studied the images, searching for any sign of the deterioration I'd missed, but found none. The first shot was of his alluringly slender back, and in the last, his grin was as easy and bright as it had ever been.

What had I missed? Kim claimed there was nothing, but how could that be true? Was addiction really so fucking illogical?

As I thought it, I realised I'd inadvertently hit the nail on the head. Logic played no part in this horrible disease. How could it, when Kim had been so happy when he'd called me that last time?

I had no answer to that, and the images of Kim filling my screen with his grace and beauty hurt my heart. I shut them down and opened up a folder I hadn't looked at in years—one of my oldest files.

The individual images opened in the sequence that I'd taken them twelve years ago, growing progressively more horrifying with each shot. I poured over them with the morbid fascination only a photographer could have with images like these. I got lost in them, making tweaks here and there, and wondering what had become of the bloodied, soot-smeared faces I'd captured that day. Wondering if the bewildered horror in their eyes had ever faded.

"That's real pain, eh?" Kim slid into the seat beside me. "Puts things in perspective."

"Hope you're not about to tell me that you have no right to have problems."

Kim shrugged, but I could tell my gruesome screen was distracting him. He leaned closer, his shoulder brushing mine. "What are these? It looks like a war zone?"

"You're close. I took these at Edgware Road twelve years ago."

Kim missed a beat, then his tired eyes widened. "7/7? The tube bombs?"

"That's the one. I was on my way to uni when people started to come up from the tracks. I tried to help at first, but there was nothing I could do."

"Fuck. I remember watching it on the news with Brix. How old was I? Nineteen? Yeah, something like that. It didn't seem real to us, though. City life never did until Brix took up with it."

"It didn't seem real to me, either. Without these, I wouldn't really remember it."

"What did you do with these after? Did they go to the papers?"

"A few." I enlarged the images I'd sent to the *Times* all those years ago. "I didn't let them pay me, though. The fees went to the memorial fund."

Kim pointed at a bloodied woman, her face burnt, her long hair stained a dark, mottled red. "I think I've seen her before."

Of all the images he could've picked out. I closed down every file except that one, and retrieved two more from a different folder. It clearly took Kim a moment to realise the photographs were all of the same woman. He frowned. "I don't get it."

"Fate," I said. "I'd been at Kings Cross early that morning, shooting some buskers for a project. I caught her by chance as she headed underground, and then again an hour later, when she came up at Edgeware. I tracked her down when I found the first image and asked if I could photograph her one last time, so I had all three images—before, during, and after. Mad, eh? She keeps all three in a drawer at her office. Says it reminds her how fragile life is."

"She ain't wrong." Kim's eyes remained fixed on the young woman.

Knowing how much time I'd lost to staring at photographs that made my nerves itch, I closed the laptop. "How did the meeting go?"

Kim shrugged. "Good, I s'pose. I feel calmer, which helps, even though it freaks me out to see so many pissheads in one place. Reminds me how far I can fall, you know?"

"There must be people who are doing well too, though?"

"A few. I like to hover near them, absorb some of their willpower."

"Does it work?"

"I think so."

"Good. Are you hungry?"

"Not really."

I nudged him. "Tough. I'm not taking you home till you've eaten."

Kim took a little persuasion, but eventually relented and ate a small breakfast that turned into a big one as his appetite returned. I watched him, still drinking my cauldron of over-sweet tea, and wondered when he'd last eaten.

Perhaps sensing that I was fretting, he pinched my cheek. "Stop worrying. I'm sorry I fucked up, but you can't let it be all you see when you look at me. It wins that way."

"It's hard not to worry. I didn't see this coming."

"And you never will. I don't, and I know it better than anyone."

"There's nothing I could've done to help you?"

"Probably not. I just need to keep fighting. Plenty of addicts win. There's no reason I can't too."

I absorbed that with a slow nod. "Can I ask you something?"

"Yes." Kim faced my gaze head on. "Always."

"I came to the cliff to look for you because Calum thought that's where you'd be. But I wasn't the first to find you. Some bikers got there before me, and they were the same ones from the jam festival. The same ones I've seen Lena with a bunch of times. Who are they?"

Kim relaxed, wiping his hands on a napkin. "Any biker you see in Porth Ewan is from the Rebel Kings MC. Other clubs can't ride here."

"Sounds dramatic."

"It's life, just not ours. Some of the Kings are good people, though. We've been inking them for years."

"They're your friends?"

"If I ever need them to be. They're more *friendly* with Lena, if you know what I mean." Kim smirked and curiosity got the better of me.

I leaned closer. "Which one?"

"The fucking *president*, of course—she deserves top tier after me. And his mate. But that's a story for another day, and probably one I'm not supposed to share."

Damn him and his discretion. But I let it go, distracted by the easiness seeping into Kim again, replacing the tension he'd woken up with.

God, it looked good on him, and hope stirred in my battered heart. The change in him from the meeting was clear to see—the fading lines of stress in his face, the upright set of his shoulders. The weight of what he'd been through in the last few days was still there, but he had a tangible grasp on it, like he was emerging from the other side of a recurring bad dream. "I believe in you."

"I know. I think that's why I didn't dig up the whiskey I buried in the strawberry patch last year."

I couldn't gauge if he was joking or not, but the sentiment wasn't lost. "I want to be there for you—*here* for you—if you'll let me."

"I couldn't push you away, even if I wanted to. I fucking love you."

"What?"

Kim looked away. "I was kinda hoping that you already knew."

I caught his chin and forced him to meet my gaze again. "Knew what?"

"That I *love* you."

I grinned like a fucking maniac, couldn't help it. "You love me?"

"Course I do. And I *really* do, Jas. This ain't the addiction bullshit messing with my head. You have to know that . . . I'm still me, with or without it."

"I *do* know that, I promise. The only reason I've been too messed up to say so is because I bloody love you too."

"Really?"

"*Yes*. Man alive, how could *you* not know?"

Kim laughed, and it was the first real humour I'd seen in him since the weekend. "Um...perhaps because we've been too busy working and fucking to get around to saying so?"

"Actually, you kinda did say so, when you called me in Bristol, but I was half-asleep, so I thought I'd dreamed it." I laughed with him, and leaned in to loll my head on his shoulder. He was warm and strong beneath me, and the faith I had in him seemed all the more real. "You're going to be okay. We both are, together. I can feel it."

Kim kissed my temple. "I feel it too. I've just gotta remember what it means."

EPILOGUE

SIX MONTHS LATER . . .

The night owl in me had always dreaded spring. My camera craved the light, but my soul preferred the gloomy dark of the colder months, the clouds, and the shadows, the wind and the rain. It suited my mood, it suited me—at least I'd thought so until my first Christmas with Kim passed, spring crept up on us, and I realised what I'd been missing. I saw the early morning sun in his face, captured it, with my eyes, then my lens, and from that moment, I knew for sure that life had never been better.

Corny?

Maybe, but it was true. Being with Kim challenged me in ways I'd never imagined, but it was the making of me.

I loved him.

Awake, asleep, always.

But perhaps never more than when I woke in the morning to find him still sleeping. It was a damn shame I was rarely up before him, and this morning was no exception. Gentle, stroking fingers on my cheek roused me, and I opened my eyes to Kim's sleepy grin, his rumpled hair, and hooded lids.

I touched his face, addicted to his unshaven jaw. But addiction remained a tainted word in our house, and the reason Kim was awake so early didn't escape me. He kissed me, the sweep of his tongue and the scrape of his teeth a promise of what would come later, and then he slid from the bed—his bed, this morning—and padded, naked, to the bathroom.

Bewitched, I watched him go, admiring the sensual sway of his slender hips, but I caught my imagination before it could call him back to bed. This morning wasn't about me, or even about us.

This morning was Kim's.

I got up and tidied the living space of the trailer. Then I threw on some clothes and ventured outside. The chickens— larger in number now—were our responsibility this week. I let them out and collected the eggs, and I was drinking dandelion tea and cooking breakfast on the outside stove when Kim slid his arms around me a little while later.

"Make a hippie of you yet, eh?"

It was a joke that never got old for Kim, *and* my brothers, who found it hilarious that I was living the very life I'd resisted all these years. "Piss off and get the plates."

Kim obeyed, and I loaded us up with omelettes and tomatoes spiked with Kim's home-grown chillies. It was probably the nicest thing I'd cooked him so far, and the thought spawned a heat in my belly that warmed my bones. Was this how it felt to be truly happy? God, I hoped so. "Do you know how many are coming this morning?"

"Not a clue. Reckon no one does until they walk up that path."

I swallowed the last of my breakfast and considered the theory. Weather allowing, Kim had been hosting a weekly

Blood Rush sponsored AA meeting at the commune for three months now, and speculating what had brought attendees to Blackbeard's Junkyard had become one of my favourite hobbies.

After breakfast, I set out the Blood Rush mugs and filled the tea urns, and then I made myself scarce, leaving Kim to his people. I shut myself away in the trailer and worked for an hour, completing more in my snatched time on Kim's patchy internet connection than I ever did at my place where I had all day to get shit done.

The irony of my newfound focus wasn't lost on me, but I didn't dwell on it. Instead, when my hour ran down, I closed my laptop and ventured outside. The meeting was just breaking up, so I drifted to the tea station and set out the cakes Laura had sent over. Kim joined me, and I took a moment to squeeze his hand over the jam tarts. "All right?"

"Aye-aye. It was a good one today. Some folk have made real progress."

I smiled. Though I knew little of what went on in the meetings, the positive effect they had on Kim was undeniable. Addiction was a lonely illness, even for Kim, who had a wider support network than most, and the camaraderie this band of misfit addicts shared made every morning I spent pouring tea worth a thousand that I'd spent alone.

The gathering drew to a natural end. Kim drove a few elderly attendees back into town while I cleared up with the help of a couple of church volunteers. We were finishing up when a car pulled onto the muddy track that led to the commune. It was too soon to be Kim, unless he'd forgotten something, and the rest of the commune's residents rarely had visitors, so I tucked the tea urn away in the shed and set off through the orchard to meet whoever it was.

I expected the postman and the box of acrylic paints Kim

had ordered the day before. My dad hopping out of the red and yellow van, less so. "What the fuck are you doing?"

My dad grinned from beneath his multicoloured flat cap. "I was on my way to ask Kim if he wanted to come to the seed fair with me. Fred gave me a lift."

Of course he had. Where else but Porth Ewan did the friendly postman pick up hitchhikers? "The seed fair in Porth Luck?"

"That's the one. I thought he might like to get some ideas for the raspberry crop."

"He doesn't have a raspberry crop. There's no room." A sad fact, but a true one. The commune was at capacity, and there was no space for new crops without sacrificing existing ones.

"Ah, well," my dad said. "I've got some ideas about that too, if you'll come for your dinner tonight."

I raised a questioning eyebrow, but my dad just shrugged and smiled a smile I'd come to recognise as a sign that he was up to something. "We can't come until late," I said. "Kim's got ink appointments until seven."

"I thought he wasn't tattooing anymore?"

"He finishes today."

"That's fine, son. Laura's at her bridge club until the evening."

The conspiratorial grin remained, but he was saved from further questioning by Kim coming home because he had absolutely forgotten something, and it turned out that he'd planned on visiting the seed fair anyway.

"You don't want to come?" he said to me.

I shook my head. I'd embraced every aspect of life with Kim except his obsession with tramping about in the mud, nursing seedlings into adulthood. Fuck that. My father could have him, even if it meant sacrificing an afternoon I'd counted on spending in bed.

My dad retreated to Kim's car. When he was out of sight, I grabbed Kim and pushed him against the most solid part of the fence. I kissed him, shoving my hands into his messy hair, twisting my fingers to give him the tiny shot of pain that riled him up so much.

His reaction didn't disappoint. He spun us around and took control, and it wasn't long before I forgot all about my father waiting by Red's hot-pink Ford KA. That's right—Kim still drove the most ridiculous car in the world.

He broke away, his heart hammering against my chest, his dick digging into my thigh. "I can stay, if you want? I'm sure your dad won't mind."

"I think he would, actually. Gaz reckons he likes you better than the rest of us."

"If that was true, it would only be because you lot don't take him seriously. You don't know how lucky you are to have a dad who cares beyond the fact that you're still breathing."

Kim spoke with humour, but his words hit home. I'd only met his father once, and the contrast with my own had been like night and day. Billy Penrose was a gruff seaman, grey and weathered, and though his love for his only son had been obvious, it had been hard to see how a man as vibrant as Kim had come from someone who had so little time for him.

I'd never met his mother, but then, he hadn't met mine, and I couldn't see that changing.

Kim left, and after gathering my laptop and laundry together, I went home—to my rented flat—and kicked about until it felt like a reasonable hour to test a newfound friendship I'd come to rely on.

Calum met me at the Sea Bell, and we sat outside nursing

pints and forging our bond—because Calum was the only soul on earth who loved someone as much as I loved Kim.

"How are the meetings going?" Calum asked over our second round.

"Good, I think." I shot an ironic glance at the pint in my hand. "He still gets excited about them, so I guess it's working for him."

"No wobbles?"

"Not that I've seen." Which scared the shit out of me when I spent too long thinking about it. I'd missed it last time—in a big way. That couldn't happen again. "The counselling is helping with that, though. And the painting."

Which led me to the other reason I'd asked Calum to meet me. I opened my laptop on the table and pulled up the folder of images I'd shot of him the previous week. Kim called Calum an angel in a bear suit, and when I'd reviewed the photos last night, I'd finally understood why. Because beneath the dark beard, broad shoulders, and brooding gaze, Calum was the sweetest bloke I'd ever met, and somehow, the images I'd shot over a couple of pints and the weathered exterior wall of the Sea Bell, had managed to capture it.

Not that Calum seemed impressed. He winced and pushed the laptop away. "What the fuck are you showing me those for?"

"Because Kim wants to paint them, well . . . paint you, as it happens, so I said I'd ask you first."

Calum sighed. "Paint them?"

"For the new workshop. We thought of a name."

"Go on."

"So you know what the commune is called, right?"

"Right . . ." Suspicion laced Calum's gaze, and I didn't blame him. Kim and Brix had worked on the much-needed expansion of Kim's workshop together, and we'd learned fast that their combined humour was about as juvenile as it came. "Let me guess: they want to paint my face as a pirate and call the place Blackbeard's Junkyard?"

"Blackheart's Drunk Beard, actually."

"Seriously?"

I laughed. "No, but they do want to use your face as a template."

Calum's face folded into as close to a scowl as it ever got. "Brix kept that quiet."

I sympathised, I really did, but Kim and Brix's vision for the new workshop was epic, and Calum's face would make it perfect...*if* one of us could persuade him he really was that hot.

Taking a chance, I chose silence as my weapon. And it worked. A moment of mutiny passed, then Calum sighed again, drawing the laptop closer. "Okay . . . hit me. How do they want to do this?"

Later that day, I met Kim at the gates to Belly Acre Farm. Kim and the mischievous grin that usually spelt trouble or sex.

Or both. "What are you up to?"

"Me?"

"Yeah." I punctuated my words with a kiss. "You look like you've put a bramble bush on my dinner chair."

"Don't judge me by your brother's behaviour. I've just had a good day. That's all."

I felt bad then, and made up for it by groping him. As you do . . . as we *did,* frequently. But, alas, our time together hadn't yet come, and so I tore myself away and preceded him inside.

Laura waited for us and dispatched Kim to help my dad bring in the first of the spring greens.

"What did you do that for? I haven't seen him all day."

"And I haven't seen you all week, so suck it up, young man, and cut those spuds for me. Besides, I want to talk to you about something before your dad comes in."

"Okaaay." I drew a pile of potatoes towards me and set about cutting them into rough cubes. "Why do I not like the sound of that?"

"Because you still carry that city way of seeing the negative in everything." Laura slid a mug of tea across the table. "But you might be right in this case, so get those spuds done while I talk, eh?"

Laura weathered my glare as she took her place at the table and folded her hands around her teacup. "Your dad and I have been talking about your grandfather's house."

"Haven Cottage?" I pictured the old fisherman's house where my paternal grandfather had lived out his last years. "I thought you were going to rent it out? Cash in on the sea views and all that?"

"We did. In fact, we even started renovating it last summer, but you know how those things go around here."

Easily distracted would be written on the tombstone of every member of my Porth Ewan family, so I could well imagine what had happened to the cottage project. And I had a horrible feeling that I knew where this was going. Laura and my dad had made no secret of the fact that Kim's participation in the barn enterprise had been the catalyst to getting it finished. "Ma, Kim doesn't have time to design and build new furniture for the cottage. He's too busy with the workshop expansion."

"Oh, I know that, honey. We were actually thinking that you and Kim would buy Haven Cottage from us."

"Buy it?"

"Yes, to live in . . . together. You can't traipse between your lonely flat and his caravan forever."

"No?"

"*No*, Jasper, you can't. I know you're happier than you've ever been, and no one is enjoying that more than your father and I, but life is for living . . . for moving forward, and you two need a home of your own."

She had a point, but I wasn't in the business of conceding so easily. "What makes you think we have the money to buy a beachfront property?"

"Common sense, dear. You still have the funds from your flat in London, don't you?"

I did, but that wasn't the point. Kim had just sunk all his capital into expanding the workshop, and there was no way on earth that he'd agree to live in a house I'd paid for. "Thanks, ma, but no thanks."

"I had a feeling you might say that. Would it help if I told you the price we're asking? Don't forget that the place was wrack and ruin when we bought it, so anything we get for it is pure profit—"

"*Ma*."

But it was no good. She named her price anyway, and the figure was low enough to thoroughly distract me from my dad and Gaz's rowdy entrance.

Perhaps I was more Manning than I cared to admit.

Kim noticed my preoccupation during dinner. He elbowed me a few times when people spoke and I failed to answer. Only the buzz of my phone saved me from explaining myself there and then.

I stepped outside. "Hello?"

A throaty chuckle set my nerves alight.

"Red?"

"It's me. How's it going, handsome?"

I smiled up at the inky night sky. Red was tearing up America with her band, and we didn't hear from her often, but her sporadic phone calls always put a smile on our faces. "All good in this hood. Want me to get Kim?"

"Not today. It's you I wanted to speak to."

"It is?" That was unusual. Our conversations were mostly short-lived, a stopgap until Kim came to the phone. Which begged the question of why she'd called me in the first place. "What's up?"

"I'm having a baby."

"Oh." That stopped me in my tracks. "Are you okay? I didn't know you were with anyone."

"I'm not. It's…an arrangement. I'm going to be a surrogate for some friends of mine."

"Oh."

"That all you have to say?"

"Um…" Like that was much better.

Lena laughed again. "You're my test run. I'm thinking of telling Kim tomorrow, unless you want to do the honours for me. What mood is he in?"

"A good one."

"So you'll do it for me?"

"For fuck's sake. Really? Why can't you do it yourself?"

"Because I'm catching a flight first thing in the morning, and him not knowing is giving me hives."

Didn't really answer my question, but the line broke up before she could speak again. Then she was gone, leaving me holding her grenade. If that was even what it was. Kim loved Lena, and he always would, but it wasn't the same as the love he'd gifted me.

I knew that.

I *knew* it.

And I knew in my heart that his reaction to her baby plans

would be the same as mine: fond bewilderment and affection for a woman who never lived a day in her life the way anyone expected her to.

It all clicked into place. I tipped my head back, absorbing the starlight, then I went back inside.

Kim glanced my way, but my dad claimed his attention before I could fill him in. He took us into his office and laid out his offer in much the same way Laura had but with added emotional blackmail. "We need to sell it to repair the roof on this place, but it would mean the world to us to keep it in the family."

"Let Gaz buy it, then," I grumbled. "Alan Sugar the Second, isn't he?"

"Your brothers already have homes."

"So do we."

"Jasper."

"*Dad.*" The echo of my conversation with Laura grated on me, and I was irritated that Kim was here to witness it. "Just leave it, okay?"

"Jas." Kim took my hand. "Hear the man out."

I glanced at him in surprise. Setting aside the financial issues, buying the cottage would eventually mean moving out of the commune, and it hadn't occurred to me that Kim would ever want to do that.

Still, I held my tongue as my dad explained his grand plan to Kim, and this time, the penny change he and Laura wanted for the cottage hit home for real.

Kim too, if his adorably surprised expression was anything to go by. "That ain't how much a cottage by the sea is worth."

"It's what it's worth to us," my dad said. "Besides, we've given both our other children property of their own. It's only Jasper who's never let us help him."

I folded my arms. "That's because I don't need your help, not because I'm ungrateful."

"We know that, son. That's why we're asking a fair price."

Fair in whose world was apparently subjective. But the discussion was over, at least for now. My dad opened a drawer in his desk and retrieved a set of keys. He tossed them to Kim. "Go take a look. See if you can't convince my son to live a little more than he has already."

Nice. I took a breath to retaliate, but Kim hustled me out. "Don't be a dick to your dad. You're lucky to have him, remember?"

Our conversation that morning flooded back to me, and I was shamed enough to think about retracing my steps, but Kim was already walking to his car.

I followed him and got in the passenger side. He gunned the comically tiny engine and peeled out of the farmyard. "If you're worried about the money, don't be. I can afford half of that price."

"Really?"

"Yeah."

I wasn't convinced, but the money was only half my concern. "What about the commune?"

"What about it? Me and Lena settled there because I'd forgotten how to live like a normal person . . . how to own things, build things, and love anything that wasn't her. But that was a long time ago. Life has changed for me, *I've* changed. And I want a future with *you*."

"What about the meetings?"

"We can host them anywhere. It ain't about the location."

I chewed on my lip and mulled over Kim's words as he drove towards the sea. I waited for him to ask for directions to Haven Cottage, but of course, he never did. Why would he, when Porth Ewan boys knew everything about everything?

He pulled up outside a few minutes later. "Sulk all you want. I'm going inside."

Sulk? Me? Was he having a fucking laugh? But as the urge to stay in the car remained strong . . . perhaps he was right. I was sulking, but why?

Who the hell knew? And who cared, when Kim was inside a deserted cottage without me?

I got out of the car and followed him inside. Knowing my family's goldfish-like attention span, I expected to find the place derelict, but I was mistaken. The interior of the cottage had fresh new plaster, shiny wood floorboards, and crooked polished beams that fairy tales were made of. An open fireplace was the crowning jewel of the lower floor, and there was even a bed and a claw-foot bathtub upstairs.

Kim was sold, I could tell.

"Red's having a baby," I blurted.

He turned around, his expression unreadable. "What?"

"Surrogate. For some friends of hers. She's flying somewhere to go to do whatever she's going to do to make that happen tomorrow."

"How do you know that?"

"She called me."

"During dinner?"

"Yeah."

Silence. My heart began a slow, painful descent into my stomach.

"Why did she call you?"

"I don't know."

"Liar."

I moved closer. "She wanted to know how you were before she told you."

"How I am?" Dangerous humour glittered in Kim's convoluted gaze. "Jesus. You two think I can't handle reality without hurling myself off the wagon? That ain't fair, Jas. You can't shelter me from the truth."

"I'm not. I'm telling you, aren't I?"

"Yeah, while you look at me like I'm an unexploded bomb. Do you really think I'm selfish enough to have my life with you and deny her the same happiness in whatever the fuck she wants to do with hers?"

"Are you happy?"

It wasn't what I'd meant to say, but whatever my intended words had been evaporated as Kim seized me by the shoulders. He pushed me hard onto the plastic-covered bed, his face a potent mix of fury and amusement. "You don't get it, do you? You have no idea how much you mean to me, even after all this time."

I had a fair idea, but I wasn't going to interrupt him while he was digging his cock into me the way he was right now. I wound my arms around his neck and pressed myself against him. "I know you love me, and I know you love her too."

"It's not the same."

"I know."

"Then how many times are we going to have this fucking conversation?"

Kim punctuated his words with a grow and flipped me onto my stomach. A thrill shot through my veins, and I shivered, my eyelids already fluttering as sensation consumed me. Time hadn't dulled the electricity between us. If anything, it had deepened, solidified, and he could bring me to my knees with the intent behind his stormy gaze.

And his intent was clear now—he was going to fuck me, and I was going to let him . . . more than that. I'd beg him if he kept me waiting.

But we weren't playing that game today—the game where he tied me with no tangible binds and drove me slowly mad with his sensuous tongue. No. This wasn't about making me crazy with need, desperate for any part of him he'd give me. This was about him, and me, *us*, and everything in between.

He shoved my jeans away and unbuttoned his own, and then with a slick of the lube we always carried, slid into me in a smooth motion that made my toes curl.

I groaned, arching my spine as the sensation of taking him bareback overwhelmed me. We'd stopped using condoms a while ago, but the ridged heat of his hard dick never got old. Each time was like the first as Kim gripped the tops of my thighs, my hips, my back, and nailed me with sharp, hard thrusts that left me in no doubt of how he felt.

If there had ever been any.

Has there? I couldn't be sure. There'd always be a place for Red—for Lena—in our world, but the part of Kim I'd believed would always belong to her, was now, unmistakably, mine.

And I was his.

Kim unravelled, my name falling from his lips as he came hard.

I wasn't far behind. And my climax was harsh, painful in all the right ways, and it wasn't until I crumpled face-first into the plastic sheeting below me that I remembered we weren't at home in my flat.

"Fuck." I laughed, giddy and high. "That didn't take long."

Kim collapsed on top of me. "Long to what? Convince you that you're stuck with me whether you like it or not?"

"I do like it." I rolled us so we could face each other. "I meant that it didn't take long to break this place in."

Kim's intense gaze brightened. "Does that mean we're doing it? Buying it from your 'rents?"

"If you want to."

"What do *you* want?"

"I want to be where you are . . . and I want a reliable

internet connection, a desk, and a bed that doesn't turn me into a ninety-year-old man overnight." Kim could sleep on a pile of rocks and still bounce out of bed in the morning. Me? Damn. The sofa bed in the trailer was just about killing me-- *don't care. I'd fucking die for him.* "And I want you to be happy."

"I *am* happy."

"I know you are, but I want you to believe you deserve it, even when things go wrong."

Kim pulled his jeans up and sat down. "You know me so well."

"Do I?"

"Yeah. I've never been able to articulate how this—" he stopped and rubbed his chest "—thing, this addiction, makes me feel, even in meetings where I know people will get it if I can just get the words out. But you get it without me saying a fucking thing. You get *me*, even if addiction makes no sense to you."

Emotion burned my eyes. "Things don't have to make sense to matter. You matter. We both do."

"Then we both deserve to be happy, right?"

"Right."

"So let's do this. We can build something amazing here, I know we can."

"We can—"

Kim's bone-crushing embrace was instant and wonderful. I fell headfirst into it, losing myself in all that was him. All that was *us*. Our journey had barely begun, and we couldn't predict the good or the bad, but together, we were ready for anything.

Thank you so much for reading Junkyard Heart! I hope you enjoyed Jas and Kim's love story.

If you're interested in the Rebel Kings MC, the entire series is available to binge on Kindle Unlimited. And yes, Rubi, Cam, Nash, and Saint are so worth it.

Join my Patreon for bonus scenes.

Find my whole catalogue on my Amazon page!

www.ingramcontent.com/pod-product-compliance
Lightning Source LLC
Chambersburg PA
CBHW021011180626
46814CB00003B/1243